Becoming Still

Becoming Still

Maria Christina Benavides

Halo
PUBLISHING
INTERNATIONAL

Halo Publishing International
7550 WIH-10 #800, PMB 2069,
San Antonio, TX 78229

First Edition, April 2024
ISBN: 978-1-63765-564-1
Library of Congress Control Number: 2024901912

Halo Publishing International is a self-publishing company that publishes adult fiction and non-fiction, children's literature, self-help, spiritual, and faith-based books. We continually strive to help authors reach their publishing goals and provide many different services that help them do so. We do not publish books that are deemed to be politically, religiously, or socially disrespectful, or books that are sexually provocative, including erotica. Halo reserves the right to refuse publication of any manuscript if it is deemed not to be in line with our principles. Do you have a book idea you would like us to consider publishing? Please visit www.halopublishing.com for more information.

Chapter 1

Dark-wash jeans; fitted, solid-black V-neck; five-o'clock shadow; tall; and handsome standing in the corner by the bar. He is looking around the bar, holding his drink. I wonder where his girlfriend could be. As handsome as he is, there is no way he is here alone. After a half an hour of slyly watching him, I gather the courage to walk over to the bar where he is standing. I ask him if there is anyone sitting on the barstool next to him. Waiting for him to speak, I am surprised when he simply shakes his head. I take a seat and notice that he inches slightly away from me.

I can feel the intensity of his thoughts radiating from him. Unsure of what has him so deep in thought, I try to start a conversation by asking what he is drinking. He stiffens next to me, but still doesn't speak. Now, thinking this was a bad idea, I try to think of a way to leave without making it obvious and awkward.

Deep in thought, I almost missed his acknowledgment to my question. I try to come back to reality and focus on what he just said, but he is already staring at me intently. Not sure of what he just told me, I stupidly reply with an "Excuse me?"

He furrows his brow and says, "Whiskey."

Feeling like an idiot, I apologize for not paying attention. This seems to intrigue him, as I was the one who asked the question, not the other way around.

"But you were the one who asked the question. Do you make it a habit of asking questions and becoming distracted before one has the chance to respond?"

Stunned by his question, I stumble with my response, "I…I normally don't, but this is new territory for me."

He raises an eyebrow. "Asking a question is new territory for you?"

Laughing, I can feel my cheeks turning bright red. "No, I ask questions and carry conversations just fine. It is the approaching strangers and asking random questions that is new territory for me."

"Oh, I see."

Unsure of what to make of the situation, I decide it's time to leave before I make a bigger idiot of myself. "I am sorry for having interrupted your thoughts and your drink. You have a good night. Excuse me." As I turned to jump off the barstool, he grabbed me by the elbow, and I froze. Slowly I turned my head to look at him, and he asked me not to go.

Acknowledging his request with a nod, I turned back around on the barstool. He asked me what I was drinking and ordered another round from the bartender. Sitting and waiting, there is still a silence between us that feels as if no amount of words can break it.

Feeling brave after having some of my drink, I lean closer to this man and ask him what has him thinking so hard and being so quiet.

He turns to face me with a shocked look on his face. "You are quite curious, aren't you? If you hadn't already told me, I would assume this is normal behavior for you."

Blushing once more, I apologize and take a sip of my drink.

He swivels in the barstool and sits facing me with one of his legs up on the rung of the stool. "An inquisitive person tends to get far in life. Are you inquisitive by day or solely when you have had something to drink?"

Taken completely by surprise, all I can do is stare at him with what I know are wide eyes. "I can assure you that I do not allow alcohol to control me. I have merely posed those questions because you look like a rather intriguing individual."

He pauses for a moment and takes a swig of his drink. After a few seconds, he turns to look at me. "You say I look like an intriguing individual, but you hardly know anything about me except what I like to drink. Can you truly judge me without further knowledge? Furthermore, why is it you are trying to judge me? Have you no other activities to occupy your mind? Is this why you came to the bar? Or did you come here seeking something else?"

Carefully cradling my drink, I lean forward. "I am not trying to judge you, and the fact that you think I am, merely tells me that you are a judgmental and egotistical man." Insulted, I jump off the barstool, chug my drink, and tell him, "I have no idea why I was so curious and intent on getting to know you. It was apparently a waste of time. Have a good night." Without hesitation, I storm out of the bar before he has another chance to grab me.

Halfway home, I realize that I left my friend Annie at the bar. I type a quick text letting her know that I have already left for the night and that I will see her at home.

Annie: *Okay. Be careful!*

I continue walking home, trying to calm down from the awful encounter with that man. I couldn't quite pinpoint why I thought he was special in the beginning, but I could feel it from across the bar and even more intensely when I made my way over to him and sat next to him. If only he hadn't been such an asshole, I could have at least put a name to such a beautiful face. *Well, maybe this will teach me not to initiate any conversations with men in bars.*

I got home and took a quick shower before heading to bed. As I was lying in bed and drifting off to sleep, I could see the handsome man's face. Try as I might, I could not get myself to sleep. His face haunted my thoughts. I lay in the darkness until the early hours of the morning.

***

As the alarm rang, I practically jumped off the bed, scared half to death. I must have fallen asleep because the last thing I remember was looking out at the half-moon. I brush my teeth, and as I look in the mirror, I see the terrible bags under my eyes. *Damn it, Christy! How could you stay up so late thinking about that man, beautiful as he may be?*

After a quick shower and getting ready for work, I run to the kitchen for some breakfast that I am pretty sure Annie is making. Annie got home shortly after I took my shower and went to bed last night.

"How was the rest of your night? I'm sorry I left so abruptly."

She smiled. "It's okay. Mike walked me home."

Michael Johnson has been my best friend since elementary school.

"Who was the man that you were talking to at the bar before you stormed off?"

I feel myself turning red. "I am not sure. I tried talking to him, but wasn't able to get anywhere. He basically told me to buzz off in a not-so-nice manner, so I gave him a piece of my mind and stormed off."

Annie can't help but start laughing. *I sound absolutely ridiculous!* It makes me look as if I became extremely emotional over a man I had only just met and stormed off like an angry girlfriend. I couldn't help but join in on Annie's laughter.

After breakfast, we head for work. Both of us are employed by Gary and Wilks Enterprises (GW). Annie is a certified public accountant, and I am a lead on the marketing team.

I was born and raised in South Texas. After graduating from high school, I felt it was time to venture out to a college or university far from my hometown. I considered my options, but ultimately found that I really wanted to go to Georgetown University to study business. I was extremely nervous about moving so far away from home, but knew it would be a great experience for me.

During the process of receiving a room assignment from Residential Living, I was paired with Annie Myers, who also happened to be from Texas. To my surprise, Annie was also studying business. We hit it off immediately and became very good friends. After four years of college, we were lucky to intern together at GW and, soon after, were hired into our current positions.

After arriving at GW Tower, we take the elevator up to our offices. Annie exits on the eighteenth floor, while I keep riding up to the nineteenth floor. As soon as I walk into the reception area, Landon is waiting for me. Landon Scott is my administrative assistant, and he is excellent at his job. Landon advises me that I have already missed three calls, and there is a meeting that I need to get to on the twentieth floor in fifteen minutes.

I thank and hug him as I run to my desk; drop my purse and tote on my chair; grab a pen, meeting organizer, and iPad; and rush upstairs to the conference room. The meeting is to update the owners, Blake Gary and Christopher Wilks, of the goings-on with their current clients.

As I walk into the conference room, I see that there are quite a few people who have not shown up yet. I find my seat next to my boss, Ana Sheffield. Ana has been with the company for a few years now. She, like Annie and me, completed an internship at GW and is now the marketing director. Waiting for everyone to join us, Ana and I engage in a conversation about potential clients.

As we are discussing an emerging company that has recently launched a new video game, Blake and Christopher walk into the conference room. Everyone moves to find their seats. Ana takes the opportunity to gain everyone's attention. She begins by discussing the minutes from the previous meeting and moves to address any concerns or comments. No attempt is made to discuss any concerns, nor are there any comments. She continues to move through the agenda and is discussing all the recently acquired clients and the status of each account.

GW recently was contracted to do a promotions campaign for a new line of diamond jewelry and a new brand of vodka. Ana explains that she will be assigning me to be the lead on the vodka campaign.

Christopher seems intrigued by the idea and addresses his question directly to me, "How do you feel about this campaign?"

With a smile, I respond, "Feeling confident."

Blake nods his agreement, and Ana continues explaining the progress of the other campaigns that are currently on the table. The meeting runs for about forty-five minutes until Blake indicates that he has another meeting to attend in half an hour.

Ana is wrapping up her report when Christopher interrupts before the meeting is adjourned. "Blake and I recently met with our old friend James. He has developed a new alcoholic beverage and has asked us to help him advertise it. We know that we have quite a few projects going on right now, but we are confident that you and the team can handle one more addition. I had my receptionist email you the details. Please let me know if you have any problems getting in contact with James. Thank you all for your time this morning and have a great day!"

Ana wraps up the meeting and dismisses everyone shortly after Blake and Christopher leave. I gather my things and begin walking to the stairwell. After the drinks and the Chinese food I had the previous night, I really need the exercise. When I was halfway down the hall, Ana called out for me. I half-turned to find her a few short steps away from me.

"Christy, I want to meet with you about the vodka campaign and a few other things. Take an early lunch, and be in my office by 12:45 p.m." Before I could say anything, she turned around and walked away.

When I got back to my office, Annie had sent me an interoffice message: *Do you want to grab lunch?*

I typed up a quick response letting her know that I had to go at 11:30 a.m. because I had to meet with Ana at 12:45 p.m.

The response was almost immediate: *Meet you at the elevator at 11:25 a.m.!*

The rest of the morning went by fairly quickly. I did research for the vodka campaign and began some of the mock-ups. I worked on some of our other projects and even put together some proposals for the other campaigns we were working on. By the time I looked up to check the time, I had to rush down to the elevator because it was 11:25 a.m. Luckily, Annie had gotten caught up on a phone call and was just walking up to the elevator as the doors opened on the eighteenth floor.

"How's your morning going?"

"More like where did my morning go?" I gasped.

"You got that right." She snorted. In a more serious tone, she asked, "Where do you want to eat today? I'm starving!"

Contemplating whether I should at least try to salvage the rest of this week by eating healthily, I decided I would just hit the gym later. "How 'bout a burger for the diet?!"

Laughing loudly, Annie agreed to my suggestion.

GW Tower is located on the corner of Eighteenth and Guadalupe Streets. Right across the street, there is a great little place known as De Mayo's, and I am absolutely in love with their Mayo burger!

After a quick lunch, Annie and I headed back to GW Tower. My meeting was scheduled for fifteen minutes from then. We rushed up to the elevator, said a quick "See ya later," and went our separate ways.

As I walked into reception, Landon gave me a few messages and advised me that Ana scheduled our meeting in the west conference room. I went to my desk and gathered the materials that I thought we would need, along with the mock-ups, and made my way to the west conference room. When I got there, the room was empty. I began setting up the mock-ups and the projector so that I could catch Ana up on everything that I had worked on.

A few minutes later, I heard Ana in the hall speaking with someone. The conference room door opened, and Ana walked in with Charlie Lewis, another marketing lead on our team.

"Hi, Christy! Wow, what's all this?"

"Hi, Charlie! I wanted to make sure I brought Ana up to speed with my accounts. Hi, Ana!"

Ana walked in and took a seat on the opposite side of the table. "Hi, Christy, I love that you came prepared! This is why I brought you and Charlie here today. Please bring me up to speed, and then we will get to the main reason for our meeting."

Surprised, I proceeded to update her.

"Wonderful, Christy! I am truly impressed with the mock-ups! Please make sure to set a meeting with Mr. Stevens and me to discuss the vodka campaign. Now, have a seat so we can discuss some pressing matters."

I did as Ana requested, still rather confused about what exactly was going on.

"Ana, can you please explain why Christy and I are both here? It feels like we are in trouble for something that neither of us are aware we did," Charlie exclaimed.

Laughing lightly, Ana responded with, "No, no, you are not in any trouble! I wanted to meet with both of you to discuss Christopher's comment this morning."

Concern etched Charlie's light-blue eyes. "Are you saying that we will actually be picking up their friend's project?" he asked.

Not that it would be impossible, but our team was currently juggling about ten other projects. To add another one would begin to spread us a bit thin. Although it probably was not a good idea, I really didn't see a way out of it since it was a request from the very men who signed our paychecks.

Ana smiled slightly. "I know you are concerned about our current workload, and to add another project is quite possibly going to spread us thin. But the fact is that Christopher and Blake have been friends with James for almost fifteen years, and they will do anything to help him. We need to make sure that this additional engagement gets the same attention the rest of our projects get."

At this point, I couldn't help but ask, "Why are Charlie and I here?"

Charlie chimed in, "Yes, why are Christy and I here?"

"You both are here because I am going to need for both of your teams to work on the campaign for James," Ana responded.

Eyes wide, Charlie and I were stunned by her declaration. In the two years I have been here, we have never worked a project jointly. "Ana, not that it bothers me, but we have never shared a project," I retorted.

"Christy is right. We have never shared a project. Why exactly are we starting now?" Charlie asked.

Ana's expression softened. "I understand that this is new territory for both of you, but in order to lighten the workload for your teams and actually provide an excellent campaign, I believe our efforts would be best served if your teams work as one on this project, instead of a single team taking the lead. You will both collaborate on this project and bring me your ideas. We have a meeting with James and his associates next Thursday. Please make sure to prepare your teams. I will email you both the details so that you can begin brainstorming."

Shortly after her declaration, Ana gathered her things and left the conference room. Not sure what to make of this, I asked, "Charlie, do you think she is doing this because she doesn't think an individual team can handle it, or do you think the reason she gave us is true?"

Charlie shook his head. "I am not quite sure, but I would prefer to acknowledge that she has our best interest at heart. I have to accept that she is having both our teams work on this so that our overall workload is lightened."

Nodding my agreement with him, we made plans to schedule a meeting with both our teams for the next morning to brief them on the situation and to start brainstorming.

The rest of the afternoon went by fairly quickly. My team and I met to discuss the current campaigns and so they could provide me with some progress notes that I could use to add to my reports. At 5:30 p.m., I gathered my things and headed for the door.

Landon was waiting for me at the elevator. "Hey, Christy! Quite the busy day, huh?"

I let out a sigh. "It sure was! I am so exhausted, but I really need to get to the gym. I had a Mayo burger for lunch, and I feel like I've committed a cardinal sin!!!"

Laughing, we both moved forward when the elevator doors opened. To our surprise, Christopher and Blake were both in the elevator. With wide smiles, Blake looked back and forth between us and then asked if we were always this excited about leaving work.

Without a filter, as always, I responded with, "Not normally, but Landon here was making fun of my regretful lunch choices."

To which Christopher let out a loud laugh! "Christy, what could you have possibly eaten that you could have such regret?"

With wide eyes, I looked at him and said, "Mayo burger from De Mayo's."

To my surprise, Blake chimed in with, "Christy, it would be a sin not to eat a Mayo burger when you go to De Mayo's! I can assure you that you should not regret anything except the fact that you went to De Mayo's and didn't invite the rest of us!"

Shocked that I was so easily having this conversation with the owners, all I could do was say, "I promise to extend the invite the next time I think about going across the street!"

On the first floor, we all went our separate ways. I met up with Annie right outside the building. She was staring intently at me with her emerald-green eyes. "Why are you looking at me like that?" I asked.

"You just got off the elevator, laughing with Christopher and Blake! Why else do you think I would be looking at you like this?!"

Laughing, I put my arm through hers and started walking toward our apartment. As we entered it, I told Annie that I really needed to hit the gym and asked her if she wanted to come with.

"After the lunch we had and the mess of drinks from last night, I definitely need to go! Give me five to get ready!"

While she changed, I grabbed some water bottles for us and packed some towels in a bag. Annie was all about the Zumba classes. I, on the other hand, was good with some cardio and weights.

At the gym, as Annie headed to the studio, I made my way up to the second floor where the elliptical machines were. About twenty minutes into my cardio session, I swore I felt someone staring at me. I paused the machine and made a nonchalant grab for my water bottle while looking around.

As I was turning from my left side to the right while taking a sip of my water, I almost spit it all out! At the end of the row, on the last treadmill, there he was…intently staring at me! I couldn't help but check him out from head to toe. He was wearing some black-and-red running shoes with matching basketball shorts and a black muscle shirt. His huge biceps glistened with sweat. And let's not forget his gorgeous face with his hair falling slightly over his forehead because it was damp from sweat.

Get ahold of yourself, Christy, and stop ogling him! Although it was too late, I caught myself, turned around, and jumped off the machine, not bothering to finish the last ten minutes of my workout. I grabbed my stuff and headed for the first floor.

Being thrown off, I wasn't sure where to go next, so I settled on working on my legs. I made my way to the leg press, and as I was setting down my stuff and prepping the machine, I felt a light touch on my arm. I turned around and found that he had followed me. Being that I was holding a forty-five-pound weight in my hands, he seemed to keep a safe distance.

"I wasn't sure it was you at first, but then you turned around and practically undressed me with your eyes!"

Shocked by his accurate description of what I'd done, I of course pushed to deny it! "Conceited much?" *Smooth, Christy, maybe he didn't hear the crack in your voice.*

"Conceited would be making an assumption instead of stating the facts."

Damn it! He totally heard the crack in your voice! Say something to change the subject, but nothing that will bring any more attention to this awkwardness. Think, Christy! Hurry up! He is staring at you like there is something wrong with you!

"Christy! Christy!!"

Startled by my name being yelled, I turned around to find Annie standing behind me with an eyebrow raised, arms crossed, and left foot tapping. "Hey, Annie, you ready to go?"

She shook her head. "No, not yet. Who is your friend?"

Realizing the beautiful stranger from the bar was still standing behind me, I turned around, set the weight down, and grabbed my stuff. When I rotated again to look at Annie, I said, "I'm not sure who this man is, but I'm ready to head out. I have a meeting in the morning that I have to prepare for." I walked off, and Annie followed.

"Christy, isn't that the guy from the bar?!"

Shaking my entire body, I said, "Yeah, that was him, but I don't know his name, and had you not gotten there when you did, I would still be standing there making an ass of myself. So thanks!"

Laughing, Annie looped her arm around mine and said, "He was totally checking you out as you walked away."

Grunting, I said, "Ugh! Great, now I'm definitely going to dream about that!"

Annie laughed even harder at that.

Chapter 2

After taking a long, hot shower, I got into bed and tried to get some sleep. About an hour passed, and I still couldn't sleep. I kept thinking about the beautiful stranger.

What are the odds that he and I both go to the same gym? Oh my gosh! How the hell am I supposed to go back there?! I just walked out of there and didn't even say one coherent phrase to him! How embarrassing is that!?

Ugh, Christy, you are such an idiot! But how could I say anything?! He was looking amazing in those basketball shorts and his body glistening with perspiration!

Damn it, Christy! Get it together, this is not going to help you go to sleep.

Tossing and turning, I finally gave up on sleep and got up at around 5:00 a.m. I decided I'd go to the gym before work. After getting dressed, I ran into Annie's room to see if she was interested in a morning gym session.

Surprisingly, she had heard me and was up and ready to go along with me. Shocked, I said, "Wow! What are you doing up?"

Throwing a towel at me, Annie said, "Shut up! It's your fault I didn't get to finish my workout last night, remember?"

Ugh! She is right. I am such an idiot! I ran to the kitchen and grabbed some bottled water and towels before we headed out.

Unnecessarily nervous, I walked into the gym doing a quick sweep before making my way upstairs for some much-needed cardio.

Nudging me, Annie asked, "Hey, Christy, how about we work on arms today?"

Absentmindedly, I responded with a quick nod. *Get it together!* I told myself. *He is not here, and even if he was, you still need to work off all those damn burgers and drinks you have been enjoying. They are catching up to you!*

After my little pep talk, I felt confident I could get through the morning workout. After about an hour and a half, Annie and I headed back to our apartment to get ready for work.

It was a full twenty-four hours before our weekend began. Annie and I planned on taking a little trip down south to visit some friends, Lilly and Aiden, over the weekend. We had been planning this for over a month. Lillian Summers, whom we met toward the end of college, was one of our closest friends, and Aiden Hamilton was her main squeeze.

"Annie, you ready to head out this weekend?"

A big smile appeared on her face, and she didn't have to say anything, but she did anyway, "Oh my gosh! I have been waiting for this weekend for what feels like forever! I can't wait to see Lilly and Aiden!"

"I am totally with you on that! Miami is going to be off the chain."

We made our way up in the elevator at GW Tower. With all of my newfound energy from the morning workout, I was absolutely ready to take on my day! Annie and I made it to work about thirty minutes before we usually strolled in, and that gave me just enough time to meet with Charlie to gather our thoughts for our joint meeting that morning in the conference room.

Charlie and I compared schedules and found that both of our teams were ahead of schedule on all of our projects. Feeling positive about where we both were with our workload, we decided to have an extended brainstorming session. Although Charlie and I had never worked on joint projects before, we both had a very similar way of working through our assigned campaigns. We decided to order in some breakfast and have it sent to the conference room. We had Landon bring in some whiteboards and plenty of beverages as well. This was going to be a good day to start on some ideas for James's account. After everything was set up, Charlie and I set off to gather our teams.

Back in the conference room, Charlie decided to begin the meeting. "Good morning, everyone! I can see the confusion and worry in your faces. I know that this is a bit of a surprise to have everyone in one meeting room without actually having a departmental meeting. Christy and I don't want you all to worry because no one is in trouble." Turning to me, Charlie motioned for me to take over.

"Good morning, everyone! Charlie and I have gathered you all here to address the needs of a new client we discussed in the departmental meeting. Christopher and Blake asked Annie to form a team to work on their friend

James's campaign. Annie felt that our teams already had plenty of work and did not want either of our teams to get spread too thin. So her solution was to combine our efforts so that both teams share the workload." Smiling at Charlie, I let him finish the introduction.

"Christy and I have reviewed our current campaigns, and we are proud to say that we are ahead of schedule! Thank you all for your hard work! Today, we are going to take advantage of our timeliness and begin brainstorming for the new account. We have sent the details to your tablets. Please review them over a pastry, and we will begin brainstorming in about fifteen minutes."

After about four hours of collaborative work, Charlie and I agreed that we all needed a break for lunch. We dismissed everyone and advised them to meet back in the conference room at 1:15 p.m. I took the elevator down to the eighteenth floor to see if Annie wanted to grab a bite to eat. I was starving and in the mood for tacos. After that morning's workout, I felt as if I could eat a horse!

Rounding the corner before Annie's office, I heard Christopher, Blake, and her having a conversation. I decided to take a seat in the small waiting area outside of her office and check my emails. About ten minutes later, they all walked out of Annie's office.

"Afternoon, Christy!" Christopher and Blake said in unison.

Startled, I looked up and saw they were all staring at me. "Good afternoon, gentlemen. Annie, I just came down to see if you were free for lunch, but I see that you are busy. Rain check?"

Blake looked at me with a wide smile. "Nonsense! Join us for lunch! Christopher and I have some questions for you as well. We would like to pick your brain."

Dumbfounded by his invitation, I responded with a simple nod and smile. On the ride down to the lobby, all I could think about was how I was not going to get to have tacos for lunch. I was going to have to figure out how to convince Lilly and Aiden to at least eat tacos once for breakfast during our visit.

When we reached the lobby, Christopher led us to the SUV sitting idle by the curb. His chauffer ushered us into it and then jumped in the driver's seat to ease us into traffic. I had only been to lunch with Christopher and Blake once before, and that was by pure coincidence. I had never been personally invited. Had the world flipped upside down, and I didn't know about it? That was twice in the past few days that I had interacted with them without it being planned or for work purposes. I really needed to snap out of it and pay attention.

Shit! Everyone is staring at me again.

Christopher spoke this time, "Christy, are you all right? We were wondering if there was something in particular you wanted for lunch."

Shaking the stupid off, I replied, "I'm sorry. No, I do not have anything in mind. I am sure whatever you all suggest will be great!"

Blake chimed in, "Well then, how about a steak? You ladies do eat steak, right?"

And to that I couldn't help but smile wide! "We're from Texas! There is nothing better than a juicy, medium-rare steak!"

Everyone started laughing as we reached one of the nicest steak houses in DC. Realizing this was going to probably be a long lunch, I excused myself to make a quick phone call to Charlie to let him know that something came up and that I would be running late, but not to wait for me. His voice was etched with concern when I told him something came up, but I was quick to assure him that everything was okay.

Charlie is one of the sweetest guys that I've probably ever met, and I can't quite figure out why he is still single. Not now, Christy! You can ponder that later. Right now, you need to get back to the table.

When I reached the table, I saw that there was another place set at the table. Not wanting to make assumptions, I thought it better to not question it.

"Oh, Christy, you're back. I hope you don't mind, but I took the liberty of ordering a rib eye for you! Don't worry. I was sure to ask for medium rare, as you indicated," Blake said, satisfied with himself.

I could feel myself turn a bright shade of red. "Thank you, Mr. Gary!"

His grey eyes turned a smoky color as he looked at me. "Christy, I hope that Christopher and I have not given you the impression that you must refer to us by our surnames. We pride ourselves in being approachable, and you referring to us by Mr. Gary and Mr. Wilks just won't do. Please, from now on, refer to us as Blake and Christopher."

Christopher turned to look at me and gave me a curt nod.

I smiled and said, "I will make a note of it Mr.— I mean, Blake."

"Good! Now, the reason Christopher and I have brought you and Annie here today is to discuss some business. You ladies have been with the company for some time, which includes your internships. We feel that you all have become tremendous assets to our company, and we hope that you feel like you are valued."

Christopher chimed in with, "Now, don't think that a free lunch is what we are talking about. You *will* be receiving a free lunch this afternoon, but Blake and I would like to offer a little bit more than that. We normally don't go around your superiors—or the HR process, for that matter—but with the incredible work you two have been doing, we didn't feel there was a need to go through the entire process. Blake and I would like to offer you both a small raise and a bonus to show our appreciation."

Flabbergasted by this admission, Annie and I stared at each other before either one of us spoke. I found my voice before Annie. "Christopher, Blake, I don't know what to say. I mean, obviously, thank you so much, but that seems meager in comparison to what you just offered us."

Finding her voice, Annie added, "Blake, Christopher, thank you so much for that offer! Christy and I are extremely grateful for the opportunities that you both have given us. We are the women you see before you because of the opportunities that were afforded us by completing the internships with your company. You have no idea what it means to us that you feel so strongly about the work we have done and will continue to do for your company."

Blake said, "I am delighted to hear that, ladies! We feel that you two will go very far in this industry. Especially because you all are so young and have accomplished so much. We are just grateful that you all decided to pursue your careers alongside us."

Christopher continued, "Now, with that out of the way, you both will need to go to HR before the end of today to complete all of the necessary paperwork."

At that moment, our food arrived. The rib eye that Blake ordered me looked amazing! It appeared that everyone was having a steak. I glanced over at the empty place next to Blake and found that the waiter had placed a steak there as well. I suppose the confusion showed on my face because, next to me, Christopher chuckled.

"The real reason we brought you two along is because we are having lunch with our friend James. He should be walking in… Ah, there he is!"

Turning to see at whom Christopher was motioning, I almost choked on the small piece of steak I put in my mouth! *Now, I know the world has flipped on its axis!* Walking toward us was the beautiful stranger from the bar and the gym! *Holy hell! He looks amazing in a suit! Christy, pull it together! This is a professional lunch meeting.*

Realizing that I might just make an ass of myself, Annie brought me back from the edge. She nudged me beneath the table, and I looked directly at her. She mouthed to me, "Relax. Everything will be all right! Just breathe in and out!" Heeding her warning, I began to take deep breaths.

Just then, James walked up to the table. Blake and Christopher both rose from their seats. As James looked around, he and I made eye contact, and at that moment, all I wanted was for the floor to open up and swallow me whole!

James said hello to Christopher and Blake, all while not breaking eye contact with me. Finally, he looked away for a brief moment as Blake introduced Annie. He took Annie's hand and kissed the top of it.

Holy smokes, could this guy be any hotter?

Then, as Christopher cleared his throat and began to introduce me, James spoke, "Hello again, Christy."

Holy shit! He knows my name?! How the hell am I going to explain this to my bosses?

Not now, Christy! Respond!

"Hi there, Mr. Still!"

Shocked by the interaction, Blake interjected, "I didn't realize you two knew each other. How long have you been acquainted?"

Trying not to let anything slip, I responded, "We actually ran into each other at the gym yesterday."

Annie must have sensed that I was drowning; she reminded us that our food was at the table and getting cold.

I really need to get this girl an expensive gift or something. I have no idea what I would ever do without her.

We spent the next fifteen minutes in silence. I made it a point to concentrate fully on my food and cutting my steak into precise one-inch pieces. Not that I ever did that, but I needed to focus my energy on something, or I would seriously lose it. Although I didn't look up from my plate, I could feel the weight of someone staring at me. Too afraid to look, I continued to stare at my plate.

I am assuming Christopher could not take the silence any longer; he cleared his throat, which pulled me out of my concentration. "So…the reason we are here is to talk logistics. Blake and I agreed to help James with his new project. However, we need you two ladies to help put this together. Annie will be handling the accounting portion of the project. Christy, I know you and Charlie are collaborating on this, but you will be the lead on this account. I want you to continue collaborating, but final decisions will be passed through you before they get to Ana or us. James, do you have any specifics that you would like for the campaign to entail?"

Looking from Christopher to me, James gave a half smile that almost looked like a smirk. "Given that this is my baby, for all intents and purposes, I want to make sure that it has a lot of qualities that embody my personality. I know that can sometimes be difficult to capture, but I have full faith in your team. I also have some other points I would like for you all to hit. Christy, may I have an email address so that I can forward those to you?"

You can do this, Christy. You are a professional. As long as you keep him at arm's length, you will be able to get through anything.

I took a business card from my purse and handed it to James. "Of course, Mr. Still! Here you are. Please feel free to email me any ideas you may have and anything that you feel will be essential to the campaign."

Perfect! That was on point, and your voice didn't even crack. You can and you will do this!

Engaging in light conversation, we finished eating. The waiter brought the bill, and Blake picked up the tab. After which, we all stood and walked out toward the SUV that was waiting at the curb.

An hour and forty-five minutes after we had left for lunch, we arrived back at GW Tower. As we took the elevator up, I exited on the nineteenth floor after thanking Blake and Christopher for lunch and excusing myself. I ran to my desk, set all of my stuff down, and walked over to the conference room.

When I walked in, Charlie immediately looked up and gave me a once-over. After realizing that I was okay, he smiled at me and waved me over. I could tell that the team was hard at work because the whiteboards hardly had any white space left, and there were piles upon piles of papers on the table. Charlie—along with Sophie, one of his team members, and Jordan, one of mine—was at the farthest whiteboard.

As I reached Charlie, I saw all of the wonderful ideas that our teams had put together. I checked my watch to make sure I had only missed thirty minutes of the afternoon brainstorming session because they were on a roll!

"Wow, guys! This is incredible! You all are on a roll!"

There were wide smiles across the board, and Jordan said, "Thanks, Christy! We did a rehash of the vodka campaign and decided that anything that worked for them, we would have to do the opposite for this."

Absolutely impressed, I said, "That's wonderful! You all reverse engineered this thing! I have some points that we need to address, things that Mr. Still wants to see in this campaign. But, otherwise, I think we are definitely on the right path."

The rest of the day flew by. Our team was absolutely pulling together great ideas, and if we kept going at this rate, we would have myriad ideas by the time we met with Mr. Still. We closed out our brainstorm session at 4:30 p.m. I made my way over to my office and gathered my messages from Landon on the way. As I reached my desk, I heard a ping from my desktop. I took a seat and opened the email tab. I saw a few new emails, but the most recent was from James. I felt my stomach turn over.

Will I ever get it together when this man's name comes up? Ugh! I really hate feeling this way.

I opened the email and saw a time and place. *Well, this is strange. He was supposed to email me the ideas he wanted us to incorporate into his campaign, not set a meeting.* Looking at the clock, I saw I only had half an hour to get across town. I gathered my belongings, ran down the hall to HR, asked for the paperwork mentioned during lunch, and headed out to try to make my meeting on time.

As I jumped into a cab, I typed out a quick text to Annie: *I have a meeting across town. I will see you at home.*

A few minutes later, a felt a light buzz.

Annie: *All right, be safe.*

So like Annie—she is always worrying about my safety. I seriously think she is going to make a wonderful mother one day.

About twenty minutes later, the taxi pulled up to the address I had been given in the email. It was a quaint little street, and the storefront appeared charming. *I wonder why James sent me here. It appears safe enough.* I paid for the taxi and made my way to the door.

As I walked inside, I found that it was not a storefront at all. The interior was set up like a bar. *I wonder if this has anything to do with his new beverage line.* I looked around, but I didn't see James anywhere. I was about to turn to leave when I felt him come up behind me. *I swear this guy is like a freaking ninja!*

Trying to keep my composure, I stepped forward and then turned around. He lifted an eyebrow, but I acted as if I didn't see it. "Hi there, Mr. Still."

He didn't respond immediately, but when he did, it threw me for a loop. "Why did you step away before you turned around?"

I honestly think my mouth dropped open at that. I had no answer for him. I really needed to get it together because he seemed to be waiting patiently for me to regain my composure. It's as if he knew the question was going to throw me off, but he felt compelled to ask it anyway. Scolding myself, I finally got it together and said, "Because I felt you rather close, and if I turned without stepping away, I might have turned straight into you."

A sly half grin appeared on his face. "Would that have been a horrible thing?"

At the rate this is going, this man will be the death of me. I keep making a fool of myself in front of him. His last question had me gawking at him.

I heard a ping from my phone that must have been my email. What a sweet distraction because it reminded me that I was here as a professional.

"Mr. Still, I presume that I am here for business purposes? Is this related to the campaign that we are handling for you?"

His playful grin disappeared, and he became very businesslike. "You are correct, Ms. Mills. I have asked you here because this is where I would like for my new beverage line to debut. I wanted you to get a feel for the place. It might help with some of the color schemes and other mock-ups your team puts together."

I chose that moment to break eye contact. I turned around and walked about the room. It was absolutely breathtaking when you actually stopped to admire it. The room had beautiful wood floors that matched the oak bar. The space had accents that could work in a variety of ways; it could easily be converted into a comfortable men-only gathering spot or a very homey place for couples to come and enjoy a nice night out with friends or family.

I got lost in the potential that I saw in this place. It almost felt as if I could see it come to life. James was right to bring me here. I opened up an enormous brainstorming session in my head. I pulled out a pen and paper, and I started writing and drawing. I was so engulfed in my ideas that I almost missed that James had gotten closer to me. If not for the unexpected warmth that I felt, I would have completely overlooked that he was standing right behind me.

My God, the energy that man emits is almost powerful enough to paralyze me. I need to make a mental note to keep a good distance between us if I ever want to get my job done.

Again, I stepped forward before I turned around to face him. "You were right to want to show me this place. It has so much to offer. I have some great ideas that I cannot wait to share with my team tomorrow. We have a few things already in the works for Thursday, but this might just give us a couple more."

I am not sure if James knew what to make of my new-found ability to not lose my cool around him, but he seemed to think better of commenting on it and said instead, "I'm glad you think so. I will anxiously await your ideas." He continued to stare at me.

After a few seconds, I couldn't take being in the same room with him anymore. "Thank you for your time, Mr. Still. I will be in touch if I have any questions. Please feel free to contact me if you have other ideas or comments that you would like to make known to our team. Have a wonderful evening."

I quickly made my way toward the door before I completely lost the little bit of composure that I had found. I could feel he was right on my heels, but I didn't stop to look back. Once I got outside the building, I hailed a cab and got in as James was walking out of the door. I caught a glimpse of him as I looked back, and I swear he was upset.

***

I made my way inside my apartment and was welcomed by the smell of a homemade dinner. Man, it had been a while since Annie and I had eaten at home. Whatever she had made smelled absolutely amazing. *I swear this girl has a sixth sense about others' needs.*

"Hey, sweets! How was your day? Dinner smells amazing!" She was just plating the food when I walked into the kitchen.

"Hey, sweetie! I figured I would make something at home since we are going to spend the weekend eating junk. How was the meeting?"

I smiled and kicked my shoes into my bedroom. "The meeting was an ambush! I was stuck in a dark room with

James…by myself! I don't know how I did it, but I made it out alive!"

Annie was in tears from laughter. "How on earth did you manage to get yourself into a situation like that?!"

I threw a towel at her! "Don't mock me, Annie! I was mortified! I swear he knows how much he affects me because the meeting started out with him teasing me. It wasn't until I received an email that I snapped into business mode. That was the only way I was able to deal with him. I figure if I can keep him at arm's length, then I can get through this. How hard could that possibly be?

"Toward the end of the meeting, he started teasing me again, and I practically ran out of there. I swear, when I got into the cab and turned back, it looked like he was upset."

Annie stopped laughing then. "Christy, did you literally run away from him?"

"Honey, I am not some rude mongrel. I said my good-byes and then walked—well, power walked—out of there before he could stop me." That had her laughing again.

Dinner was incredible! I washed the dishes and put away the leftovers in the freezer since we were leaving in the morning and wouldn't be back until Monday.

"Have you packed for the trip, Christy?"

I finished drying the dishes and turned around. "Nope! Not one thing."

Annie looked horrified. "Christy! You need to hurry up. Get everything ready because we will be leaving at 4:00 a.m.!"

I laughed! "Don't worry so much, Annie; you are going to age before you're even ready to! I know exactly what I'm going to take. I just haven't placed it in the suitcase. If it makes you feel better, you can come watch me pack."

She shook her head and excused herself to go to bed.

I went into my room and pulled out my old suitcase. I sent a quick text to Lilly to let her know I was super excited and couldn't wait to see them tomorrow. She sent me a few emojis, told me she couldn't wait either, and she would pick us up at the airport. I finished packing and went to bed. I quickly fell asleep. That might be because the last two nights had been sleepless.

***

My alarm rang at 3:00 a.m., and I was so excited I turned on music and was dancing in the shower. Thirty minutes later, I was out in the kitchen, packing some travel snacks, when Annie walked out of her bedroom and let me know the cab was downstairs.

This was going to be a great weekend. Lilly and Aiden lived in Miami, Florida. Aiden got a new job out there after college, and Lilly also found a position at a local elementary school. Every time I spoke to them, they sounded full of life and so happy that it was infectious.

The sun was out and there was a light, cool breeze in the air when we arrived in Miami. It was still early, and we had a four-day weekend! As soon as we walked off the plane, Lilly was jumping up and down next to Aiden and waving us down. I ran into one of her huge hugs! We jumped up and down for a minute before we let each other go. I switched and gave Aiden a giant squeeze, and they helped us with our luggage.

"I am so glad you girls made it safely," said Aiden.

"We are so excited you all were able to make it out here. We know your jobs are very demanding," Lilly chimed in.

"We are so excited to be here, and we have been counting down the days for this weekend! Thanks for having us," exclaimed Annie.

It was a short flight. It had been a little while since we had seen our friends. They used to live in a little apartment;

they now had a beautiful, two-story waterfront home. *I am so proud of my friends. They went against all odds and are now doing so great for themselves. I can only hope that Annie and I will someday find our other halves and settle in beautiful homes as well.*

"Your home is absolutely beautiful, guys! I am so happy for you all! I'm very happy we were able to make this work! I missed you guys entirely too much!" I said.

We had a group hug.

"We miss you guys too! It's been way too long since we have been in the same city! Hopefully, we can make up for it this weekend. Come, let's have you ladies freshen up so we can go have some breakfast and do some shopping!" said Lilly.

They showed us to our rooms. I was dressed in workout clothes, so I decided to rinse my body, change into a sundress, and put my hair into a messy ponytail. I wore a bikini underneath just in case. *After all, we are in Miami.* Satisfied with my outfit, I made my way downstairs. Everyone was already ready to go.

"Sorry, I know I'm always the last one to finish getting ready."

Everyone started laughing, and Lilly said, "It's all right, sweetie; we know, and it doesn't mean we love you any less. Let's hurry, though, because the place we are going to brunch gets packed really fast. I hope you all are hungry because this place is the absolute best!"

We all jumped in the car, and Aiden drove us down the beach to a little place that was just off the coast. It was absolutely beautiful. It was only 10:30 a.m., but there was already a line outside. We got in the queue, and a waitress came by to take drink orders. This place was so cute; I could definitely see why it was so popular.

Fifteen minutes later, the hostess found us a cozy little booth by the water. We sat and discussed the menu options. We talked about old times and all of the mischief we got into when we were in college. We laughed and ate so much our stomachs hurt; we didn't know if it was because of the food or the laughter.

When Aiden excused himself to go to the bathroom, Lilly didn't skip a beat. "So…any hotties in your lives? Come on; spill it!"

I laughed, and Annie blushed a little. She said, "I haven't met anyone."

Then Lilly turned to me. "What about you?"

I laughed a little more. "Girl, you know I have absolutely no game! If Annie doesn't have anyone, I sure as hell don't!"

Annie gawked at me, and Lilly caught on very fast. "Don't lie to me! Annie seems to think there is someone hanging around."

I scowled at Annie. "A few weeks ago, we went out, and I exchanged words with some guy who was not interested. But it turns out that he is best friends with our bosses, and now I have to handle a campaign for him. He turns up everywhere, and there are very blurred lines about our acquaintance."

Annie shook her head. "You make it sound like there is nothing there. The night at the bar started something that has been growing since. Then, you see him at the gym… and at the lunch meeting…and then again last night. These last two weeks have been all about him. He has this energy about him that attracts you, and you can't seem to get away."

I couldn't believe Annie ratted me out.

Lilly was jumping with joy in her seat. "Do you have a picture of him? I can't believe all this has happened, and you haven't said a word!"

I shook my head. "I do not have a picture of my client, and nothing is going on. He is a client, and I am being a professional."

Lilly and Annie burst out laughing uncontrollably as Aiden walked up to the table. "What's so funny?"

I shook my head. "Oh, you know these two hyenas are always ganging up on me and think it's hilarious when I don't know how to properly respond to awkward situations."

Aiden laughed and told them to leave me alone. We finished up with brunch and left the little bistro. We headed to the boardwalk to do some shopping before we hit the beach. As we approached the boardwalk, Aiden pulled up to the front instead of parking and said, "All right, ladies, you all have fun. I am going to go for some golf, and I will swing by and pick you all up around 4:30 p.m. Have fun!"

If there was one thing I loved about Aiden it was that he always knew when to quit the conversation—or in this case, the situation. We thanked him for dropping us off and told him we would see him in a few hours.

The girls and I made our way into town for some retail therapy. If it was one thing the three of us were good at, it was shopping as if it were a job. We were all very frugal too. I don't think any of us actually ever paid full price for anything. We spent the afternoon going in and out of shops, trying on clothes, and being silly with sunglasses and hats.

After we did some window shopping, we made our way down to the beach and found the perfect spot with some beach chairs and a bar nearby. We picked up some drinks, headed over to the beach chairs, sat, and enjoyed being out by the water, relaxing, and drinking. Life was good when I had my two sisters around me. These girls were amazing, and I was absolutely grateful that God put them in my life.

Chapter 3

At about 4:00 p.m., we began making our way back to the boardwalk where Aiden had dropped us off. We were walking in and out of shops, and by the time we got to the front of the boardwalk, Aiden was just pulling up. We headed back to the house to get washed up and rest before we went out for dinner and dancing.

When we got home, I jumped in the shower and soaked under the cool water for a little while. After finishing up, I wandered into the bedroom to pick something to wear. I sat on the bed and closed my eyes for a minute, but I ended up drifting off.

***

I walk into the gym and head up the stairs to the elliptical machines. I start my workout and feel a tingling sensation on the back of my neck. Don't stray from your workout, *I tell myself, but the sensation becomes stronger and stronger. I finally give in and turn around to find James on the machine behind me; he is watching me intently.*

OH MY GOD! This man is seriously hot, and I cannot stand the way he is looking at me when all I'm trying to do is work off my damn unhealthy eating habits!

I must have a deer-in-the-headlights look because he gives me a sexy-as-hell smile and a wink before he comes to a halt in his workout.

"Ms. Mills, I didn't realize that was you. How are you this morning?"

I don't know what this man is playing at, but why must he be on the machine right behind me when there are twenty other machines on this floor of the gym?!

"Good morning, Mr. Still. I am doing well; thank you for asking. May you have a great workout and a great day!"

I begin to walk away, but am jolted backward. I can feel the warmth of his touch, and the scent of his perspiration is intoxicating.

"Not so fast. You always run away from me, and I don't understand why. You were the one who started this when you

approached me at the bar. Tell me what you were looking for then. Why do you keep running from me?"

I am frozen in place, and I assume he knows that because he turns me around to face him. He tips my chin up so that I am looking at him when he repeats, "Honey, talk to me. Tell me what you were looking for that night." He tucks a stray hair behind my ear and runs his thumb down my jawline—

***

"Christy! Christy, wake up!"

I opened my eyes just as Annie was throwing a pillow at me. I shook my head and threw the pillow back at her.

"All right, all right! I'm up! Why must you always throw pillows at me?"

I got up, checked my phone, and saw that it was 5:45 p.m. I had slept for almost an hour. *Goodness gracious, what is with that dream?!* I had to get James out of my head because nothing good could come of this since I was the lead on his campaign.

Annie pulled me out of my thoughts with, "And what were you dreaming about? You had a huge smile on your face before I threw the pillow at you!"

I stuck my tongue out at her and said, "I have no idea. Do you remember all of your dreams?"

She laughed and told me to get ready because she was starving.

I rummaged through my luggage and found my favorite royal-blue V-neck dress. I tried it on, and it looked great! I loved this dress because it fit just right. It hugged all of my curves in just the right way and accented my double Ds just enough to tease. *Tonight is going to be so much fun!* I finished getting ready and walked down the stairs to find everyone waiting for me in the living room.

Aiden looked up as I rounded the corner, and his jaw dropped. "What the hell are you wearing?! You aren't leaving the house like that!"

I laughed. Aiden was always acting like the big brother.

The girls turned around, and both of them whistled. "Damn, girl! Where are you going, and why didn't we get the invite?" said Annie.

Lilly chimed in, "Who are you looking to attract tonight? You'd think you would want to save that for a night out in DC."

I shook my head. "All right, guys, relax! You all are wearing amazing dresses as well! Why am I the one that's getting all this fuss?"

Annie was wearing a beautiful yellow dress that was backless, and Lilly was wearing a coral dress that dipped very low in the front and was also backless. We all laughed and headed out the door.

Miami was amazing during the day, but at night it was breathtaking. The skyline was beautiful, and the waterfront with the stars shining bright was absolutely incredible! Aiden drove us to one of the fancy restaurants downtown, and the line that was outside was ridiculously long. *This place must be where it's at because I can't believe the line of people that are waiting to get in.*

Aiden pulled up to the valet stand, and they helped us exit the vehicle. I thought we were going to make our way toward the end of the line, but we walked straight to the front of it. Apparently, the people in line were waiting just in case reservations fell through or people cancelled. Lilly told us that Aiden made the reservation the minute we agreed to visit them two months ago.

"Lilly, this place is amazing! I can see why everyone is waiting outside just in case."

She smiled. "We have been wanting to come here since it opened last year, but the waiting period to get a reservation is ridiculous. When you all agreed to come down, we decided there was no better reason to try again."

Aiden walked back toward us, after checking in with the doorman, and said, "Our table is ready. Let's follow the hostess."

As we walked through the dining area, I couldn't help but admire the beautiful chandeliers that hung from the ceiling and the art on the walls. We reached our table, which was in a secluded area of the restaurant. This section had warm colors and a little fireplace. It was peaceful and rather quiet, as compared to the main dining room. When we were seated, the hostess said our waiter would be with us shortly.

Annie was admiring everything around her. "Aiden, how on earth did you score this beautiful little nook? I thought we would definitely be out in the main dining area."

Aiden looked just as surprised as we were. "I didn't do this, but I'm definitely not complaining."

We giggled and proceeded to look over the menu. When the waiter arrived, we ordered our drinks and some appetizers.

"How are you guys enjoying living in Florida? Is it everything you imagined?"

Aiden smiled, but it was Lilly who answered, "Florida is great. We love living here, but it's hard being so far away from family and friends. We've made new friends, and they are wonderful people, but it's not the same without you all." It almost looked as if she was going to cry.

Aiden put his arm around Lilly and said, "We would have told you all before, but we figured we would wait until you got here. We have both gotten new positions in DC. I will be working at Howard University, and Lilly has gotten a position within the District of Columbia Public School System. We will be moving back to DC in June."

Annie and I were speechless for what seemed like a really long time. Finally, I snapped out of it, jumped up from my chair, and went to hug them both! "OH MY GOD!!! I am so excited right now! This is definitely cause for celebration!"

We had a group hug, and Annie finally found her voice, "I cannot believe you all have been holding on to this news! When did you all find out that you were moving back?"

Lilly and Aiden laughed and said they found out the previous month and were so tempted to tell us, but thought better of it. They decided to wait until we visited, so we would have something to celebrate.

The dinner was amazing. I, of course, had a steak, medium rare, and everyone else had salmon and shrimp. We topped off our dinner with dessert. It was a delicate lemon cream cake with a dusting of powdered sugar.

"Dinner was amazing, guys! Where are we going to continue this celebration?"

We made our way out to the valet stand, and Lilly said, "A new club opened up recently, and we thought we would hit that up. It's supposed to be a really fun time."

"It sounds like we are going to have an epic night!" I said.

The car pulled up, and we rode off. When we pulled up at the club, it didn't look like much from the outside, but again there was a long line of people waiting to get in. We used the valet again, and when we were helped out of the vehicle, the valet asked Aiden his name. It was strange, but he gave him his name, and the gentleman told him to head directly to the front of the line.

We all looked at each other, but we didn't argue. Maybe we were just having great luck. We walked inside, and the space was exquisite. It was elegant, but warm at the same time. They were playing the top forty in the main bar, and there was a room for salsa and merengue. This was proving to be a great place.

"I'm going to go get us some drinks at the bar. You ladies find us a table," Aiden said.

The girls and I wandered around, taking everything in, and we found a table near the back wall. This was a usual spot for us; we all loved the back walls because, from there, you get a full view of everyone in the place.

After a few drinks, I was feeling the warmth spread throughout my body. I could feel the music reverberate through me, so I grabbed Lilly and Annie by the hand and dragged them onto the dance floor. We danced a few songs, downed another shot, and headed back out onto the dance floor. Aiden joined Lilly, and Annie found a suitable dance partner as well.

I, on the other hand, was dancing solo. I felt amazing for a while, but then I sensed a tingling down the back of my neck. I thought I was daydreaming because, I swear, it felt just as it had in my dream. I ignored it and kept dancing, shaking up against Annie and Lilly and then returning to my solo dance. The tingling sensation became stronger, but I kept ignoring it.

I felt a pair of hands on my waist and turned around to find some cute guy behind me. I danced with him, and he started running his hands up and down my sides. Suddenly, I didn't feel his hands anymore. I turned around to see a tall man facing the cute guy who was holding his hands up before he turned away.

Who the hell is this guy, and what gives him the right to run dudes away?

I tapped him on the shoulder to get his attention. When he turned around, I nearly fainted. It was James Still. I gaped at him. What the devil was he doing in Miami, much less in the same exact club I was in? I abruptly turned, walked away from him, and headed toward the door. He was on my heels, but didn't make an attempt to stop me.

When I got outside, I turned right and walked away from everyone. I figured James would follow me.

Sure enough, James was behind me. After I was a good distance from the people in line, so they couldn't hear, I turned around. "What the hell gives you the right to interrupt my dance? Wait—that's not even the most important question. What the hell are you doing here in the exact same place I am? How did you even know how to find me? I can't even comprehend what is going on right now. Why? Ugh!!!" I shook my head because I just didn't understand what was going on. My thoughts were a mess.

James took a cautious step toward me and said, "First, you look incredible tonight. Second, I am in Miami because today is the grand opening of my club." He motioned toward the club behind us. "Third, I interrupted your dance because that guy was disrespecting you. I may have overstepped my bounds, but I can assure you I was only trying to protect you, Ms. Mills."

I seriously could not understand or make sense of anything that was coming out of his mouth. And did he just call me Ms. Mills after he told me I looked incredible? *What the fuck?* Did he seriously just "protect" me on a professional level?

"Mr. Still, I can assure you that all we were doing was dancing, and if I felt disrespected, I would have handled the situation myself."

He relaxed his stance and said, "Ms. Mills, although I do not underestimate your ability to protect yourself, you have had a few drinks, and your judgment may be impaired. You and your friends have enjoyed yourselves tonight, and that is not a problem. However, you all used my valet, and, unfortunately, I cannot let you drive yourselves home. When you all are ready to leave, I will have a car take you where you need to go. Now, please rejoin your group and continue enjoying your evening."

He motioned for me to move toward the club's door, and I seriously didn't even know how to argue with that.

I was so confused that I just could not think coherently. I didn't respond to him. I simply followed his lead and walked toward the club. When inside, I saw my friends at the table, and I walked toward them. I didn't realize that James was following me.

When I reached the table, Annie was shocked, and Lilly was wide-eyed, while Aiden went on the defensive. "Christy, are you all right, sweetheart?"

I nodded my head and then noticed the girls' expressions. I looked over my shoulder and saw James standing there protectively behind me.

He spoke at that point, "Ms. Myers, wonderful to see you again. I hope you and your friends are enjoying yourselves at my newly opened establishment." Then he turned to acknowledge Lilly and Aiden. "Good evening, my name is James Still; it is a pleasure to meet you. I am a business acquaintance of Ms. Mills and Ms. Myers, and I am also the owner of this club."

I saw Aiden visibly relax and Lilly's face light up. *Oh dear Lord, she is not going to let me live this down.* I jumped in before Lilly could run wild. "Mr. Still has kindly offered to have a car drive us home since we have had too many drinks tonight. We do not have to leave just now, but once we are ready, he will have the car waiting for us outside."

Despite my deflection, Lilly was not deterred. "Mr. Still, would you care to join us for a drink?"

I think James felt me tense up because I heard him chuckle and say, "As much as I would love to, I must get back to work. It was a pleasure, and if you need anything, please do not hesitate to ask. Ms. Myers, Ms. Mills, enjoy the rest of your night." He excused himself and walked away.

As promised, Mr. Still had one of his cars drive us home and our vehicle delivered. I was way too buzzed to ponder the goings-on of the night. I took a shower, got into bed, and passed out.

I woke up the next morning and thought it was all a horrible dream. I wandered downstairs to put some coffee on and found Annie already making breakfast. She looked at me and started laughing. That's when I knew it was not a dream.

"Annie, what the fuck happened last night?!" I slumped in a chair, and she brought me a mug of coffee.

"Sweetie, I couldn't explain it even if I wanted to. However, he was such a gentleman, and that earned him points with Aiden and Lilly."

Dear Lord, what the hell am I going to do?

I was sitting there, taking in the aroma of the coffee and the warmth it brought me, when my phone buzzed. I looked over and saw a message from a number I didn't recognize. I opened it.

Good morning, I hope you slept well. Maybe when you get back to DC, we can discuss what happened last night.

I didn't even have to ask how he got my number. This man is such a mystery, and I feel as if I am getting myself into very deep waters with him. I typed a quick response and turned back to Annie, who was watching me intently.

"Who was that, Christy?"

I couldn't lie to her. "It was Mr. Still. He wants to discuss what happened last night when I get back to DC."

Annie beamed with excitement. "Are you still going to sit there and tell yourself and me that there is nothing going on between the two of you?"

I took a sip of my coffee and nodded…because I knew, if I spoke, my voice would give me away.

Just then, Lilly walked into the room and found Annie making breakfast. She seemed ready to fuss about it, but then thought better of it. When we were in college, Annie was our chef. She made sure that we were always fed. Even though we were in Lilly's home, Annie couldn't be kept out of the kitchen. Lilly took the stool next to me and grabbed a mug of coffee that Annie had set down for her. Aiden walked in shortly after, and he did the same, sitting next to Lilly.

We ate breakfast and decided to go down to the beach for a while. Lilly and Aiden's home had a beautiful backyard that was beachfront. We wandered out there after breakfast. I decided to take a book and a blanket to use under the umbrella they had pitched. I wasn't much of a swimmer, so I mainly just enjoyed the sun and the cool sea breeze. Annie went for a walk, and Lilly and Aiden went for a swim.

I was relaxing under the umbrella when I heard a ping come from my phone. I sat up and pulled it out of my bag. An email from Christopher appeared on my screen.

Hello, Christy and Annie,

I hope your weekend trip is going wonderfully. I am sorry to bother you, but Blake and I would like to meet with you and Annie when you get back from your trip. May you all enjoy the rest of your day and have safe travels home.

Until then,

Christopher

Just as I was thinking, *Well, this is strange. Why would they want to meet with us again?* Annie walked up to me and sat on the blanket.

"Did you get the email?"

I nodded. "What do you think it could be about? We never get emails over the weekend."

She shook her head and said, "Maybe we should just take it easy the rest of the weekend. Who knows what Christopher and Blake have planned."

I agree, "Let me send them a response so we know at what time and where." I type a quick reply to the email and ask for details of the meeting.

Lilly and Aiden walked up and asked us what we wanted to do today. We told them about the email we received from our boss and that we had decided to stay in tonight and relax. They agreed, so we spent the day lounging around and packing up some of the stuff from their home since June was right around the corner. There were so many memories hidden in their home, and it was such a delight to share them again.

Aiden went out to pick up a pizza and some beer for dinner. While he was gone, Lilly took full advantage of the time to ask me about James. "Christy, spill it! You have been avoiding the elephant in the room all day, and I know it's because of Aiden."

I shook my head, but knew I couldn't get away with it. "Okay, fine. Annie and I went to a bar about a week ago, and we were with a decent-sized crowd. I was scouting the place and laid eyes on this guy. He was dressed in dark-wash jeans and a solid-black V-neck. He had a five-o'clock shadow and an air about him that just caught my attention." Just thinking about that night made me shiver all over.

"It took me a minute to decide whether I wanted to talk to him or not, but I finally got the courage to walk over there. He was brooding, but he had this sexiness about him. I tried talking to him, but he wasn't in the mood. He was judgmental and egotistical, so I gave him a piece of my mind and stormed out. Just like that, he pissed me off within twenty minutes.

"I didn't see him again until a few days ago. I was at the gym, and I felt someone staring at me. I looked around and found him at the end of the room; he was just watching me. I jumped off the machine and went downstairs to work on legs. When I got to the leg-press machine, he showed up right behind me. He said he didn't know it was me until I undressed him with my eyes."

I started laughing, and the girls shook their heads, but were very into the story, so I continued, "Annie came by and saved the day. The next day, we were going to go to lunch when Christopher and Blake caught us and invited us to eat with them. When we got to the restaurant, I saw there was an extra place setting and was too polite to ask. I went to the bathroom, and when I came back, I saw they had ordered food for the empty chair. I was about to ask who was joining us when James walked in. Dumbfounded, I failed to acknowledge or even hear what Christopher and Blake were saying." I paused and shook my head, still reeling from that day.

Annie decided to chime in, "Oh my God, he was so polite it was panty-dropping. He even kissed my hand when he introduced himself."

Lilly wiggled with the joy she got from the story. "He sounds like an absolute keeper, Christy! So what happened last night?"

I had been keeping myself busy to avoid thinking about it, but now I was going to have to spill and process at the same time. "I am not certain what happened with the cute guy, but when I stormed outside, James followed me. We got outside, and I was so confused I asked all the wrong questions. He then proceeded to compliment me and continued to refer to me as Ms. Mills. I had no damn idea whether he was being personal or professional." I put my head on Lilly's lap.

She played with my hair and said, "I know it's confusing, love, but it seems that he genuinely cares about you. Did he say as much last night when you spoke with him?"

I lay there for a minute and then remembered. "He said the guy was disrespecting me and that he may have overstepped his bounds, but he was just trying to protect me. Do you think he was sincere about that? I mean, he did have someone drive us home to make sure we made it home safely."

I could see Annie smile, and then she said, "He also texted you this morning to see how you were doing."

"I seriously have no idea what is going on, and I am truly scared of heading down the wrong path."

Aiden walked through the door and saw me lying on Lilly's lap. "Oh Lord, what happened? Is everything all right?"

We all laughed, and Lilly answered him, "Yes, everything is okay; we are just having some girl talk. Is the beer cold?"

Aiden let out a sigh and nodded. He left the pizza on the coffee table with the beer and went into the kitchen to get some plates and napkins.

We turned on a movie, ate, and drank until about midnight. Annie and I realized what time it was, so we helped clean up and made our way to bed. I didn't take a shower since I took one when we got back from the beach, and I was going to need one in the morning to help wake me up. The food and the beer helped me go straight to sleep.

* * *

My alarm went off at about 7:00 a.m. I woke up and went for a morning jog. To my surprise, Lilly was already up and at the door, waiting for me. When we were in college, we would wake up after our escapades and go sweat out all the junk that we drank the night before. We jogged about a mile and a half before we decided to go back home and get some coffee and breakfast.

After a quick shower, I decided on another sundress and messy ponytail. It was Sunday, after all. We took another day to take in the sights and help pack up some more things before Annie and I started packing our bags for our Monday departure. We all went to bed early since our flight was scheduled for 7:00 a.m.

* * *

I realized I only brought sundresses to Florida, so I threw on another one and made my way downstairs. Traveling really didn't call for anything more. I could pass myself off as business appropriate in a sundress. After I finished getting ready, I packed up all my stuff and headed down the stairs.

Annie, as always, was slaving away in the kitchen. She made her famous waffles. As I made my way to the breakfast bar, she winked at me, and I knew she made this breakfast for me! Waffles are my absolute favorite, and they also double as my comfort food.

As if he'd sensed my state of mind, my phone buzzed, and I looked down to see it was a message from James.

Good morning, may you have a safe flight! I look forward to meeting with you later.

My stomach was in knots. I thought he would at least give me a few days to get rid of the jet lag and get my thoughts together. I picked up my phone and typed out my response.

Good morning, Mr. Still. Thank you for the well-wishes. I am not opposed to meeting with you to discuss the weekend, but I am afraid today will not work for me. How about another day this week?

I set my phone down, and almost instantly it buzzed again.

Ms. Still, I am afraid there is not much choice in the matter. See you later.

What the devil did that mean? I figured I would just not respond because I was afraid, if I did, I would receive another cryptic message; I just couldn't take another one of those.

We finished breakfast and drove to the airport.

Chapter 4

At the airport, we said our goodbyes and told Aiden and Lilly to let us know when they scheduled their move so we could ask for a few days off to help them. We went through airport security and boarded the plane.

When we landed in DC, Annie shook me because I had dozed off. I wiped the sleep from my eyes, checked myself in the mirror to make sure I didn't look hideous, deplaned, and made our way to the arrivals-pickup section. Annie and I never checked any bags for fear that they would not make it to our destination. We packed what we needed and bought whatever we forgot when we reached our destination.

We walked through the airport exit and saw Christopher waiting by his town car. He waved us down.

"Good morning, ladies! How was the flight?"

We smiled and walked toward him. "Good morning, Christopher, our flight went well. Thank you for picking us up," I said.

He smiled and his driver took our luggage and placed it in the trunk. We got into the car and found that Blake was in the car as well. "Good morning, ladies! I take it the flight went well?"

Annie was the one who responded this time, "Good morning, Blake, our flight went well. Thank you."

Christopher joined us, and we made our way out of the airport. Blake spoke this time, "Well, I imagine you ladies are wondering why we arranged this while you are still on vacation, of all things, and especially when you are fresh off a flight." He chuckled.

Christopher picked up where he left off, "You see, we would like you all to be fully aware of what we meant when we said you have become great assets to our company. Blake and I have picked up word that our greatest competitor is looking to snatch you up."

Annie and I looked at each other and then to Blake.

He nodded and continued, "Christopher is correct. Annie, you are an absolute genius with our books. Even when we feel like we are on the verge of crossing a line, you fix it and keep us just far enough away from that, so we don't. Christy, your ideas and the way you approach clients is revolutionary. We have found that our clients seek you out instead of Ana. That is not to say that Ana doesn't do a wonderful job. You just have a way about you, and, well, the truth is we cannot afford to lose either of you." Both of them shook their heads as if they couldn't stand the thought.

Annie and I stared at each other, and then I spoke, "Blake, Christopher, I can assure you that it is news to us that anyone else is interested in our work. However, I can say with absolute certainty that Annie and I have no desire to go work for anyone else. You both believed in us when no one else did. You gave us an opportunity when not even your competitors did, and for that, we are eternally grateful." Annie nodded her agreement.

Christopher smiled wide and said, "We are very happy to hear that! We want to take you gals on a little trip this coming weekend. I hope you all don't have any plans because this will entail a little bit of work and a little bit of fun. As you know, Blake and I own quite a few businesses, and we would like for you all to get a feel for what those are. We would like to give you a bit more responsibility— that is, if you all would like that, of course."

We must have looked as if we were two deer caught in the headlights because both of them started laughing, and Blake said, "You do not have to respond to that just yet. For now, just enjoy the ride. We are going to do a little bit of business, and then we will take you ladies home."

We rode in silence for a little while. Staring out the window, I saw a sign that indicated we were heading toward Great Falls. *Oh Lord, am I even dressed to be heading out there?* I looked at Blake and Christopher, and they were dressed in polo shirts and pleated shorts. *I think I can pull off wearing a sundress. Why the hell are we going to Great Falls anyway? Both Blake and Christopher live in the city.*

OH MY GOD!!! Panic set in as we turned into an estate driveway. *Please tell me this is not James's home.* I could feel my stomach in my throat. *This is going to be a very long day.* I looked at Annie for support, but she was in conversation with Blake. *Breathe, Christy! It's going to be okay; just breathe.*

I think Christopher caught on to my wariness because he placed a hand on my shoulder and asked if I was okay.

I smiled and nodded. "Yes, thank you. I believe I just need to stretch my legs and get some fresh air, is all. The plane was very stuffy."

He laughed. "I know exactly what you mean. We are here, so you can stretch and get some of that fresh air."

I can do this. Plus, what if this isn't his house? Yeah, I'm sure this isn't his house. Why are we even here anyway?

The driver came around the car and opened my door. I waited for Christopher to exit before I stepped out. He helped me out of the car, and a nice breeze hit my face. It was exactly what I needed to help snap me out of—

I am certain my mouth dropped open. James was walking down the stairs of the estate, and he looked absolutely gorgeous! He was wearing a fitted white V-neck that really displayed his muscular arms and black jeans that fit like a second skin.

Annie bumped me from behind, and I snapped my mouth shut. I shuffled over to the side and turned to look at her. She was giggling like a little girl. I shook my head and remembered I needed to breathe.

"Christy, pull yourself together! He is walking toward us, and you're standing there looking like an idiot! I know you are freaking out and probably on the verge of a panic attack, sweetie, but inhale and exhale deeply!"

I took her advice and began inhaling and exhaling in a calm manner. It took a little bit, but I leveled out my breathing, and the panic began subsiding. It happened just in time because James reached us at that exact moment.

"Hello there, everyone! How was the drive up here? Ladies, how was the flight?"

Blake took the lead on greetings. "Good morning, James! Thanks for the invitation to the estate! The girls had a safe, but stuffy, flight. Do you think they could freshen up inside before we head out?"

James turned to us, leaned in, and gave Annie a kiss on the cheek. Then, he turned to me and gave me a kiss on the cheek as well, but his lips lingered on my skin. Their warmth was exquisite.

"Absolutely. Marcus will take your luggage upstairs. Why don't you all follow me for some refreshments and snacks."

We let the men lead the way. Annie bumped shoulders with me and gave me a wink as we walked up the stairs.

The architecture of the house was enchanting. The front doors were massive and made of dark-brown oak. We entered, and it was not at all what I imagined as I stood outside. It was so warm and inviting—ironic, since James seemed so uptight. His home did not match his exterior at all. We made our way to a living area that was prepped with finger foods and beverages.

Annie and I had just reached for a sandwich when I felt a hand on the small of my back. I turned, and James was at my side.

"Marcus has brought in your luggage and placed it in one of the guest bedrooms. I hope you ladies don't mind, but I advised him to put both suitcases in the same room. I figured you all would be more comfortable that way." I nodded, and he pointed toward the door. "Marcus will show you where you ladies can freshen up."

Annie and I smiled and excused ourselves. We followed Marcus through the house until we reached a staircase.

"Ladies, you will find your luggage in the room to the left at the top of the stairs. If you need any assistance, please feel free to let me know." He excused himself and vanished before we had time to react.

We wandered up the stairs, taking in the art. When we reached the top of the stairs, we saw there was a long hall that had an abundance of doors. My curiosity almost got the best of me, but Annie caught me by the arm before I had a chance to wander off. She shook her head and pulled me toward the door that Marcus had indicated. Annie opened the door with me in tow. The room was gigantic, and the bed was enormous.

"I think we could fit our entire apartment in here and still have a yard to go with it."

Annie burst out laughing. "I swear, Christy, you say the dumbest stuff sometimes." Still laughing, she spotted our luggage at the foot of the bed.

"Are you going to change, Annie?"

She looked in the floor-length mirror and nodded.

I was thinking the same, but didn't want to make it seem as if I was changing just because of where we were. Luckily, just in case, I always packed a more conservative outfit. It was a classy emerald-colored dress with a sweetheart neckline. I matched it with some black flats. Annie chose to go with a coral wrap dress and some royal-blue flats. We put some product in our hair and a bit of mascara to liven up our faces. Neither of us was big on makeup, but we did use it when called for. Satisfied with our appearance, we made our way back downstairs.

We had kept the men waiting for quite some time. When we walked through the door, they all stood from their seats. If I didn't know any better, I would think that Blake had a thing for Annie. I could have sworn his jaw dropped when he saw her, but he quickly recovered. I watched all three of them, and I couldn't help but notice that James, too, snapped his jaw shut. He almost looked upset when he saw us. I know that is strange, but that is the feeling I got. Not to mention his jaw muscles were flexing—a dead giveaway that James was tense.

I was going to comment on the tension, but thought better of it. Instead, I went for the appreciative comment. "Thank you so much, Mr. Still, for allowing Annie and me to freshen up in one of your guest bedrooms. It was much needed after the long morning. You have a lovely home."

He simply nodded—I assume because he was unable to speak due to the throbbing vein just below his jaw.

Christopher was the one who interjected at that point, "Ladies, you all look lovely as ever. We are going to go for a boat ride. James here would like to run some ideas by you for the campaign."

Annie loved being out on the water. I think she was a fish in another life because this girl could be in the water all day and still be completely happy. I, on the other hand, could not swim to save my life, and although I loved being near or in water, the idea of deep water scared the life out of me. I was going to have to try really hard not to lose my cool while out on this boat ride.

Annie was literally jumping for joy next to me. "I love the water! This is going to be so much fun!"

All three men laughed. James, it appeared, had finally regained his composure because he spoke after that. "Shall we?" he said as he pointed toward the back end of the house, and Christopher took the lead.

The backyard was amazing! It opened straight into what looked like the ocean, but obviously it was just a very vast part of the Potomac River. The view was incredible, and the breeze coming off the water was delectable. Christopher, Blake, and Annie were walking rather fast toward the dock, but I was enjoying the view and the breeze too much. I took my time, stopped, and even closed my eyes for a minute just to be in the moment for a little while longer. It wasn't until I felt warmth behind me that I realized James had been walking behind me the entire time.

"Beautiful, isn't it? It is days like today that make me appreciate this," he whispered in my ear. The velvet of his voice gave me goose bumps, but I still didn't open my eyes. I knew I had to be very careful today, but the moment was too good to pass up.

It wasn't until I heard Annie's laugh that I opened my eyes and realized they had already reached the dock. Blake was throwing water up at her. I didn't respond to James. I didn't want to ruin the moment, so I just began walking, and he fell in sync next to me. We reached the dock, and when we boarded the boat, my heart began to race just a bit.

Christopher was very in tune with me today because he pulled James aside, and I believe he must have asked if he had life jackets because, the next thing I knew, James was walking toward me with one in hand. I had no idea how to put one of those things on.

I suppose it was written all over my face because, when James reached where I was sitting, he knelt down, gave me a malicious grin, and said, "I won't let anything happen to you, but I know it will make you feel better if you have one of these on. Lift your arms." He moved very quickly and fastened the vest with ease. He winked at me, stood, and walked away.

I looked over at Christopher, who was holding two thumbs up. I couldn't help but laugh. I mouthed a thank-you, and he gave me a megawatt smile.

Annie came and sat next to me. "Isn't this amazing?! I love being out on the water."

I looked over at her and smiled. "It is incredible."

She giggled. "I won't let anything happen to you, sweetheart."

To that, I couldn't help but laugh. "Thanks, love!"

She looked a bit confused. "Why are you laughing?"

I controlled my reaction and leaned into whisper, "I believe Mr. Still beat you to that catchphrase."

Now, Annie was the one laughing.

"If we didn't know any better, we would think you ladies were laughing at us," said Blake.

I gave him a big smile and said, "Never!"

I hadn't gotten the chance in the last three years at GW to spend personal time with Christopher or Blake. They are really sweet guys. I have to admit, though, this outing seems to be blurring the line between business and pleasure.

James was maneuvering the boat with the ease of expertise. I was still nervous about being out in deep water, but something about being with these four people relaxed me a little. When we reached what I assume was the desired destination, James cut the engine.

He turned to us and said, "Here we are. Look around. Tell me what you see."

The others stood to take in the view. I was still trying to get my sea legs under me, so I remained seated and just swiveled to take in my surroundings. We were a good distance away from all of the waterfront estates. In fact, they looked tiny, but I knew they weren't. I was turned almost all the way around when a shadow was cast over me.

I turned to find James behind me with a hand outstretched. I shook my head. I didn't think my legs were sturdy enough to support me just yet. He cocked his head to the side and urged me once more to take his hand. I turned toward him and put my hand in his. He gripped my hand and gently pulled me forward. When I stumbled, he held on to my hand harder and caught me by the opposite elbow. Once he was certain I was standing firmly on my own two feet, he let go of my elbow and pulled me by the hand toward the front of the boat.

"Take a look, Ms. Mills. Tell me what you see."

For a second, I contemplated if he was losing his mind. *What the hell did he mean by* "Tell me what you see"*? I see water! All around me!*

But I didn't think James had meant it literally, so I closed my eyes for a second and imagined his beverage. My assumption was that he wanted Annie and me out here to talk about that.

I reopened my eyes, and I saw warm colors. I saw the way the sun hit the water at the perfect angle, which reflected a brilliant amber color. Being the marketer that I am, I pulled out my pen and notebook. I started writing down my ideas. I even drew a picture. I was no Picasso, but you could make it out.

"There you two are."

I looked up to see Blake walking toward us.

"What are you all doing over here? James, seriously, what are we doing out here if not just for fun?"

Everyone migrated toward us. I hadn't realized, but James had been leaning against the rail, facing away from the view, his arms crossed. His V-neck looked as if it would rip under the stress of his flexed muscles.

"Ms. Myers, tell me what you saw when you looked around."

Annie cocked her head slightly to the right and said, "I saw tiny houses at very far distances; I know they are large mansions. I also noticed the warmth of colors all around us. Is that close to what you were looking for? I feel like this is a test that is rigged." She pouted.

James smiled at her. "Ms. Myers, there are no right or wrong answers; there is only perception. Life is full of perceptions with few facts. I brought you all out here to see if you could envision what I want for my campaign. Christopher, Blake, what did you see?"

They looked at each other and exchanged quizzical looks. I don't think I had ever seen my bosses confused, but they quite literally were at a loss. Blake responded, "We are not quite sure what you mean, James. We see water and lots of it."

I laughed, and it wasn't one of those "oops" laughs either; it was a full-on laugh that came from the diaphragm. Everyone turned to look at me, and I covered my mouth with my hand and blushed. Everyone joined in on the laughter.

Christopher was the next one who spoke, "Care to share what is so funny?"

I stopped laughing. "I am sorry. Don't think I am laughing at you. I am actually laughing at the irony. I am absolutely terrified of being out on the water, but you all are the ones complaining that you don't understand why we're are out here surrounded by so much of it. I think

Mr. Still brought us out here so that we could revel in the beauty that is cast before us."

Everyone wore quizzical expressions on their faces, except for James.

I shook my head and continued, "Okay, for instance, take a look behind me. Do you see at the very end of your field of vision where the water and the sun meet?"

They nodded.

"What color do you see at that point?"

They looked at each other, and Annie started with, "I see a brown color."

Blake followed and said, "I see a light-brown color."

Christopher took a little longer, but said he also saw the brown color.

I smiled. "All right, how does that color make you feel? What does it remind you of?"

We were back to the puzzled looks.

"Come on, Annie! I know you can come up with something."

She blushed. "It reminds me of hardwood floors, the kind we have been looking for."

I smiled because I knew exactly what she was talking about.

Christopher and Blake still looked a little confused, but both chimed in with their responses. Christopher was reminded of damp sand, and Blake said he thought it reminded him of someone's eye color. The responses expressed the chords that were strummed by a single color.

I smiled as they waited for my response. "Each one of you mentioned something that touched you. You chose those things because they meant or mean something to you. I believe Mr. Still wants his patrons to experience similar feelings when they see or drink his whiskey."

That caught everyone's attention. Not once had anyone mentioned what kind of beverage was being introduced. Christopher and Blake turned to look at James, who was very relaxed. He looked as if nothing had just happened.

"James, is that what you are going to be selling? How come you told Christy, but didn't tell us," said Christopher.

Mr. Still turned to face Christopher. "I didn't tell her, Chris. I brought you all out here to see if you could see what I saw. I wanted to see if you got the same kind of inspiration that I got the first time I came out here. Ms. Mills is very intuitive. You two should feel honored that she is on your payroll. I didn't even drop a hint."

* * *

Annie and I made it back home in the late afternoon. We had contemplated going to the gym, but thought better of it. Instead, we stayed in, ordered takeout, and watched a movie. The trip to Florida was incredible, but it was so nice to be back home. A little past nine, I picked up the remains of our dinner and excused myself for the evening. It had been a long day, and I was longing for my bed.

Today was rather surreal. The thought of spending personal time with the owners of GW would have never crossed my mind. And then there was the matter of Mr. Still. I have no idea what his play is, but he is so confusing. I had made notes of everything that was detailed today so that I could share it all with Charlie tomorrow. It was going to be a long day since we had to present our progress to three of our clients and then spend the afternoon working on Mr. Still's campaign. As soon as my head hit the pillow I was out.

The next few days flew by rather quickly. Charlie and I were making real headway with our campaigns. We were even ahead of schedule on a few.

When the weekend came around, Michael called and asked if we wanted to go out and have a little fun. Annie and I thought it over and decided it was a good idea. We met up at one of the local bars. Michael was already there with Luke Wilder and John Simmons. Those were his two best friends from college. Michael and Luke studied architecture, while John studied engineering. They all worked for prestigious global companies. These boys were always traveling, so anytime we were able to hang out, we made the most of it.

When we first saw them, Luke grabbed me up into a bear hug! I hadn't seen him in a few weeks, and I could tell he'd missed me. Luke and I had hit it off great when Michael first introduced us. I had a little crush on him, and sometimes it felt as if the feeling was mutual. He put me down and gave me a kiss on the cheek that left me feeling warm all over. I said hi to Michael and John, and Luke bought us the first round. We hung around the bar for a while, and when a pool table became available, we wandered over that way.

I love playing pool, and Michael loves challenging me. It was sort of a habit from when we were younger. Michael and I grew up in a small town in Texas. There was never much to do, but when we had time to hang out, we played a few rounds of billiards.

After two games of pool and a few drinks, Annie and I wanted to dance; we were swaying in our spots. The boys finally gave in and said we could move on to a dance club. We walked a few blocks down and ended up at a top-forty dance club. It was early, so the lines were short.

We walked in and made our way to a table near the back, but close to the dance floor. The guys knew how to dance, but weren't much for dancing unless they were trying to impress someone. The waitress came around, and we ordered another round. Annie and I ran to the bathroom to freshen up before things got too crowded. When we got back to the table, we found John paying for some shots.

I looked at Annie and said, "Oh Lord, it's going to be a long night!"

She laughed and pulled me by the arm toward the table.

"Ladies, to our lives and the greatness we shall accomplish!" John cheered.

We clinked our glasses together and downed the shots. That was just what Annie and I needed to dance right onto the dance floor. The music was great, and there were just enough people on the dance floor that it didn't feel awkward, but not so many that there was not enough room to dance. We danced a few songs and watched the guys order a few more drinks.

"You all look like you are having a great time," Luke whispered in my ear.

I smiled and turned to whisper back, "Sure are. Are you?" I pulled away just in time to see a sultry look in his eyes. I got chills.

With a wink, he said, "Always, when I'm watching you."

I could never tell with Luke—is he interested or not?—but when he said stuff like that, it was pretty hard to dismiss. I took another shot and wandered onto the dance floor again. This time, Luke followed me.

We danced a few songs, and when a salsa song came on, a circle formed around us. I had never really danced with Luke, but we had a chemistry that was undeniable. When the song ended, Luke dipped me and kissed me on the cheek. Everyone cheered around us, and he spun me toward the table.

When we got back, I could see Michael had a grimace on his face. I moseyed over to him and leaned in for a hug. He could never say no to me. He uncrossed his arms and brought me in for a hug.

I placed my head on his shoulder and asked, "What's wrong, brother?"

He looked down at me and shook his head. That was his tell. Every time I did something he did not approve of, he did the same thing.

I rubbed his back and asked again, "What's wrong?"

He looked at me and said, "You know it's not a good idea. I don't want you getting hurt. I know you are both adults, but I seriously don't know what I would do if he hurts you."

I squeezed him and said, "Mike, don't worry so much. We are both adults, and if we wish to engage in something, it's of our own free will. We would never put you in a position where you would need to do anything. Trust in that, okay?"

He gave me a squeeze and said, "Fine, but you better use a condom. I don't want nieces or nephews running around right now."

I couldn't help but start laughing. I punched him on the shoulder and mumbled, "Dumbass."

Annie grabbed me and motioned toward the bathroom. When we made it inside, she turned to face me. "What on earth are you doing, Christy?"

I was a bit taken aback by her question. "What are you talking about, Annie?"

She crossed her arms and stared me down.

I quickly caught on to her line of thought. "I'm not doing anything wrong, sweets. I am enjoying a friend's company. Plus, it's not like I am in a relationship or anything."

She shook her head. "I know you are not in a relationship. But you know there is something serious going on, and you can't just jump around like that."

I smiled at her and rubbed her arms. "Annie, I appreciate your concern, but I am a single woman. If there was something going on, I would not disrespect it. But in the current moment, there is nothing going on, and I am free to do as I wish."

Annie shook her head and said, "All right, but don't say I didn't warn you."

The rest of the night we drank and danced a little more. We all got out on the dance floor, and when Luke spun me, I saw Annie and Mike all snuggled up and swaying from side to side. *Talk about hypocrites!* I would have to talk to both of them just as they had lectured me a few hours ago.

The rest of the night was so much fun, and we all wandered out of the bar in pairs. John met a charming lady whom he was treating to breakfast. Luke hinted that he wanted for us to go for a walk, but after Annie's and Mike's glares and harsh words, I decided better of it and gave him a good-night kiss on the cheek before Annie and I jumped into a cab.

"I think you made the right decision not leaving with Luke," she said.

I turned to look at her, but she was staring out the window. I nodded even though she couldn't see me. I knew she was right, but the look in Luke's eyes when I wished him a good night was stuck in my head. He looked as if he was genuinely hurt.

Chapter 5

"Christy! Christy!! Wake up, for crying out loud!!!!"

I rubbed the sleep out of my eyes to find myself nose to nose with Annie. "What the devil are you yelling about, Annie!?"

She shook my shoulders to make sure I was awake. "Luke is here! He looks like he hasn't slept all night. Go deal with your mess, Christy."

I pulled on a T-shirt and threw a pillow at Annie. I walked down the hall and into the living room, where Luke was pacing. He looked beautiful in a T-shirt and jeans. I had never seen him in casual clothes like that.

When he heard me walk in, Luke ran up to me and pulled me into a bear hug.

"Hey, buddy, what's going on? You look like hell. Did you not sleep last night?"

He let go of me and took a few steps back. "I thought we had something going last night, Christy. I always feel like, when we meet up, something will finally happen between us. Last night was fantastic, and I thought that maybe our chemistry had peaked, and we would finally push past the friend zone."

I looked at him as if he had lost his mind. "Luke, I love you dearly, and for a time, I thought exactly what you just said. But that time has since passed. I still love you, but that love does not exceed friendship. For many years, I wished you would pick up on the hints I was dropping, but somehow you never did. I knew I wasn't being subtle, so I chalked it up to you not wanting to push the boundaries."

He stayed quiet for a bit. Paced a bit more before staring out the window. "I made a promise a long time ago to Mike that I would never let anything happen to you. For years, I've worked on keeping that promise. One of the ways was by keeping my feelings to myself. I have always intended to keep that promise. I'm sorry I crossed the line."

I stilled, not knowing what to do with that information. *Why would Michael ask him to promise something like that?* I wanted to err on the side of caution and not ask, but at this point, I didn't think it would hurt anything. "What do you mean you promised Mike that you would never let anything happen to me?"

Luke turned away from the window to look at me. "Christy, whether you want to admit it or not, you are very important to our circle of friends. You are extremely intelligent, but sometimes you do things that aren't very smart. When I came into this group of friends, you were pretty wild, and Mike was concerned that if he walked away to hook up with someone, you would do the same with some lowlife or worse. So rather than take any chances, he made John and me promise that we would watch over you…always."

I couldn't believe Michael had gone to such extremes, but the truth is that I had gone through a pretty rough patch when we were in college. I can't imagine what being on the other side of the coin must have been like.

"I appreciate you keeping your promise all these years. I know it must not have been easy. I thought leaving last night was best for both of us, but I didn't realize our chemistry had evolved into something else. I hope that we can move forward without this changing our friendship, Luke. I really value our friendship and how easy it is."

He wrapped his arms tightly around me. "Baby, nothing could change our friendship." We stayed that way for a few more minutes until my stomach growled.

He let out a laugh and said, "How about we get you fed because I know how you get when you reach hangry status. Annie!!! Come have breakfast with us!"

***

The rest of the day passed by pretty fast. Annie and I went to get mani-pedis and did some shopping while we were at it. She questioned me tirelessly about what happened with Luke, and I decided it was for the best that I left everything where it was and didn't gossip. She was a bit upset, but understood where I was coming from. We got some great deals on some really cute dresses, which inspired us to call some of our girlfriends for a girls' night out. We made it home, got dressed, and met up with the girls for dinner.

Stacy Sherman and Ella Rodriguez were two of our closest friends. We met them our junior year of college and had been through some rough times together. Our bond was very distinct, and our friendship was like no other. It was rare for us to get together after college, but when we did, everyone needed to step aside because we always caused a little bit of chaos.

Dinner was incredible, and we lingered afterwards, having a few drinks while we debated where to go for the night. Ella suggested we go to Flasks. It was a new up-and-coming club that was supposed to be the best in town.

It was early enough that the line to get in shouldn't be too long. We paid the bill and caught a cab downtown.

When we pulled up to Flasks, a line was beginning to form outside. The wait to get in wasn't too bad, and when we got inside, it was well worth the wait. The place was fancy, but not so fancy you felt as if you couldn't let loose. The music was just right for the type of night the girls and I wanted to have.

After a few shots, we were feeling vibrant, and the crowd was just getting good. We made our way onto the dance floor. We had no filter when dancing, and we always enjoyed ourselves. We were bumping and grinding, and it never failed to attract the attention of some good-looking men. A blue-eyed, blond guy got ahold of Stacy, and a green-eyed, brunet grabbed on to Ella.

Annie and I thought they were doing well for themselves, so we headed to the bathroom to break the seal. Although we didn't like going to the bathroom this early in the night, I couldn't hold it any longer. After freshening up, we headed to the bar to down another shot and then made our way back onto the dance floor.

When we reached Stacy and Ella, my jam came on, and Annie and I jumped for joy! We started jumping around and dancing with each other when two guys came up and started dancing with us. They were handsome and knew how to dance. We danced a few songs with them before heading back to our table. When we got to the table, the waitress had another round of shots waiting for us. However, there were eight shot glasses instead of four.

I looked back and saw the guy I had been dancing with pay the waitress. When he approached, he grabbed a shot, raised the glass up for a toast, and said, "Here's to having fun!" We clinked our glasses together and knocked back the shots.

When I put the shot glass down, I immediately recalled the conversation I had with Luke this afternoon. This was one of those stupid things he had referred to. I made a mental note that I would not be going home with anyone but Annie tonight. I felt a hand on my shoulder, and I turned around to find the handsome stranger asking me to dance. I agreed, as I didn't feel there was any harm in dancing. But I kept my head as clear as the alcohol would allow so I didn't get myself into any trouble.

The music was blaring, and you could tell that the people around us were having a wonderful time. Everyone was jumping up and down with the music and gulping shots left and right. Stacy, Ella, and Annie were having a blast. I could see it in their faces.

I, on the other hand, was struggling to have a good time. I was a bit tense since I realized that this guy was looking for a good time. I danced with him because I didn't want to be the Debbie Downer of the group, nor did I want the girls to lose their dance partners because I dissed one of the guys.

A slow R & B song came on, and I motioned to walk off the dance floor. Handsome Guy had other plans. He pulled me back, placed his hands on my hips, and started to sway back and forth. It was innocent enough, so I went along with it. We danced like that for a little bit, but then his hands started to roam. I kept grabbing his hands and placing them back on my hips. I tried to create some distance by putting my hands on his chest, but he took that as an invitation to grab my ass. He had a firm grip, and as much as I pushed, he grabbed me harder.

Finally, he won, and I was back in his embrace. He had one hand on my ass, and his other hand started making its way toward the hem of my dress. I slapped his hand away, and he grabbed my hand and attempted to reach again. This time, I was pulled back by the waist before he had a chance to pull my dress up.

I looked up to see James. He set me down slightly behind him and then motioned to the guy to head off the dance floor. The guy got aggressive, and James told him they could take it outside. I looked around to see if Annie was aware of what was going on, but she was making out with this guy's friend. James grabbed me by the waist and walked me out with him while following the guy.

When we reached the patio area, the guy turned around and started yelling at James, "What the fuck is your problem, man?! You can't just walk up and take my girl from me like that! We were in the middle of something!"

James pushed me behind him, crossed his arms, and shook his head. In a calm tone, he said, "I can assure you that, one, she is most certainly not your girl, and, two, you were definitely not in the middle of anything. From what I could see, she was desperately trying to get rid of you. When a lady says no, then it means no! Now, since you cannot take a hint, I have asked my security team to escort you off my property and consider yourself banned from this establishment."

The guy looked as if he wanted to argue, but then he seemed to think better of it and turned to walk away.

I was not even surprised that this club belonged to James. It had a similar feel to the one in Miami. *What on earth am I going to do?* I seriously tried to keep myself out of trouble this time, but I guess I should have set my boundaries prior to taking all of those shots. *Damn it, Christy! You really need to get your shit together!*

James watched as the guy was escorted off the property, and then he turned to face me. He had a disappointed look in his eyes, and I didn't think I was sober enough to hear what he was about to say. This time, I had no excuse though. So, whatever James was going to dish out, I was just going to stand here and take it.

James uncrossed his arms and grabbed my hand. He pulled me back into the club and down a narrow hallway. When we reached the end of it, he entered a PIN into a keypad, and a door opened into a modern, well-lit office with a couch. He walked me to the couch, watched me sit, and then went to the mini fridge and brought me back a bottled water. "Drink," he said.

I didn't argue. I drank about half the bottle before I looked up at him again. James was leaning against the desk in front of me and just watching me.

When I set the bottle down, he motioned to me. "Are you all right?"

That caught me off guard. It was not what I was expecting to hear from him, so all I could do was nod.

"Good, now can you explain to me why it is that this is the second time I have had to step in to save you from idiots? I know for a fact that you are an extremely brilliant woman, but these encounters are leading me to question your judgment, Ms. Mills."

He was so right that I couldn't respond. *What can I counter with? I don't know why he happens to be the one who has been there to save me, but I sure am grateful for it.* I shook my head and looked down at my lap. I could feel his gaze burning a hole through me, but I couldn't stand to look at him. The embarrassment of this whole situation was quickly sobering me up.

I sat there a few moments longer, and then I looked up and said, "Mr. Still, I greatly appreciate the kindness you have bestowed upon me. I realize that I have placed myself in situations that are poor in judgment, and I plan to learn from these situations. I apologize for any inconvenience this has caused you." I stood and made a motion toward the door.

Before I could get near the door, he pulled me back by the waist. "Oh no, you don't! You will not be getting off that easy." He spun me around and pulled my chin up so that I was looking directly at him. "Ms. Mills, you are clearly not sober enough to have a meaningful conversation. I will have my driver take you and your friends home. Your tab has been taken care of, and here is your credit card. Your friends are waiting for you out on the patio, and Seth is ready to take you ladies home." He rubbed my cheek and then removed his hands. He walked toward the door and motioned for me to exit.

As promised, the girls were outside waiting for us; they were all wide-eyed. James gave Seth his instructions, and we all climbed into the vehicle.

When Seth closed the door, Stacy turned to look at me. "Christy, what the hell is going on?"

I shook my head and leaned back in my seat.

Annie snuggled up next to me and said, "It's been a long night, ladies. Let's just go home and get some rest."

I knew the girls had questions, but I just really couldn't get into it right then because, to be quite honest, I couldn't answer their questions.

***

I heard a light beeping, but I was still between sleep and consciousness. I wasn't sure if I was dreaming or if something was actually beeping. I didn't move, but then I heard it again. This time, it was a little louder. Then, I realized they were text messages.

I rolled over and reached for my phone. The sun was shining brightly, which led me to believe it was almost noon. When I unlocked my phone, I saw that it was 11:30 a.m. I checked my message app and saw that I had three messages from James. *Dear Lord! So it wasn't a dream after all.*

I clicked on his name and they read as follows:

Good morning! Did you sleep well?

I take it you haven't woken up yet.

Let me know once you wake up.

I pulled a pillow over my head and let out a light scream. *Goodness gracious. Can I say that I lost my phone, and it was dead, so I couldn't locate it? Is that too dramatic? Ugh!*

I decided to roll out of bed and take a shower before I responded. It was too early for my brain to fully function.

After I showered and had a cup of coffee, I picked up my phone and responded: *Good morning! Considering the amount of alcohol I consumed, I believe I slept decently. Did you sleep well?*

That sounded so stupid, but this was really awkward. How could I keep putting myself in situations where my client had to save me? *How immature can you be, Christy Mills?!*

My phone beeped again.

I was not able to sleep as comfortably as I would have liked, but decent enough. I am sorry to hear that you didn't rest well. You should get your rest. We have a meeting tomorrow at 8AM. Drink lots of fluids.

I had forgotten about the progress meeting that Charlie had set up for Monday. *For crying out loud! How the hell am I going to face him tomorrow? I don't even know how to respond to him right now. I'm so damned embarrassed. At least he reminded me to hydrate!*

I texted back: *Thank you! I will see you tomorrow!*

I spent the rest of the day bumming around. Annie had asked me to go with her to the gym, but I really was not in the mood. Aside from the hangover from hell, I felt horrible about my behavior over the weekend. As James instructed, I drank a lot of fluids. I watched mindless TV for a while and thought it best to turn in early since I did have that meeting first thing in the morning.

***

My alarm woke me at around 5:00 a.m. I didn't normally wake up that early, but after the foolishness from the weekend, I thought it would be a good idea to look my best today. I took a shower, fixed my hair and makeup, and chose a classy emerald dress with a quarter-sleeve white blazer to go along with it. I wasn't much for high heels, but this dress required at least a small pump. Once I was ready, I looked at myself in the mirror and decided I looked good enough to take on the world.

I walked into the kitchen to find Annie making breakfast. She turned to look at me and did a double take when she saw me. "Whoa!!! Where are you off to?"

I started laughing. Annie was one to always dress as I did today, but I was more into business casual than girlie business. "I have a progress meeting that James was kind enough to remind me about yesterday when he was checking in on me to make sure I didn't die of alcohol poisoning."

That did her in; she all but dropped to the floor from laughter. "Christy, you don't have to go overboard with your attire to make sure James forgets about Saturday night."

I shook my head at the memories of that night. I don't know how I would have reacted had James not been there when that guy actually pushed his luck. I shuddered. I didn't even want to think about it. I just thanked the good Lord for keeping an eye on me.

"I know I don't have to, but wearing this outfit makes me feel like I can take on the world!" I stood in my Superman pose, and Annie threw a dish towel at me. We both started laughing.

After breakfast, I brushed my teeth, and we headed off to work. We normally stopped for coffee, but I had to get to work early, so I made my way to the office while Annie made the pit stop for us.

When I got to the office, Landon had everything prepped and ready in the conference room. He had bought breakfast pastries, fruit, coffee, and juice. I absolutely loved my assistant! He was always going the extra mile to make me look good! I had to remember to buy him something special.

Charlie walked in shortly after me, and we started prepping the presentation boards. I had taken the lead shortly after my trip to Miami when James revealed his vision to Christopher, Blake, and me. Charlie was very pleased with the route we had taken, and I was grateful for the support that he showed me when putting this presentation together. We had a few options for James, and we were hoping he would like one of them, so we could begin actual production.

As we were putting everything together, our team members began trickling in. Ana walked over and reviewed the options we had laid out. She was in awe. "You all outdid yourselves with these! I am so proud of you! I am certain Mr. Still will love them!" She gave us a quick hug and made her way to her seat.

We finished setting up just before Christopher, Blake, and James walked through the door; they were deep in conversation. But, the minute they rounded the corner and came into the room, James made eye contact with me, and I swear he gave me a once-over. When he lifted his gaze, there was a look in his eyes that gave me chills.

I shivered a little bit, and Charlie asked me if I was okay. I giggled and said, "I am. I just caught a draft when the AC kicked on." He thought about it for a second and then shrugged.

Everyone found their places, and Ana motioned me to start the meeting.

"Good morning, everyone! Thank you for taking the time to join us this morning for show-and-tell. Charlie and I would like to take this time to thank our team; they have worked very diligently in putting this presentation together.

"A few weeks ago, our marketing division was tasked with producing a campaign for something we knew nothing about, except that it was liquor. We had minimal information about the product and absolutely no direction. This, however, did not stop our brilliant people from pitching their ideas. Everyone in here has imbibed their fair share, so preconceived notions were formed.

"One day, I was blessed with the opportunity to have a meet and greet with Mr. James Still. On said day, I was able to not only gather information about the campaign, but also to learn about the man behind the bottle.

"We hope that you like what you see, Mr. Still. Without further ado, Charlie Lewis will begin the presentation."

I stepped aside and let Charlie take the floor. I couldn't help but notice how the vein in James's jaw was throbbing when I talked about the day on the lake. *Did I upset him? Christopher and Blake didn't seem irritated by the mention. I wonder what the deal is.*

Charlie did an excellent job presenting the boards. He was methodical in how he presented, and he purposely ended with my favorite proposal. I carefully studied Christopher, Blake, and James throughout the explanation of the three different options, and they all nodded appropriately, but they had good poker faces. Not one of them gave a hint as to whether or not they liked any of the proposals.

When Charlie finished presenting, he said, "Does anyone have any questions or comments?"

Christopher took the lead. "Thank you, everyone, for your dedication and determination in putting these proposals together on such short notice. I think you all did a brilliant job!"

Blake nodded, but Mr. Still gave no sign of disgust or appreciation.

Man, does he have a poker face!

"James, what do you think?" asked Blake.

I could see James's eyes moving from board to board. It felt like an eternity before he spoke. "Good morning, everyone, I would like to thank you all for graciously taking on a last-minute project. I am thoroughly impressed in the quality of work this team is capable of producing. Chris, Blake, you are truly blessed to have such talented individuals working under you. Before I go ahead and select one of the options you all have proposed, I wonder if Mr. Lewis and Ms. Mills could select their preferred options and tell me why."

Christopher and Blake automatically agreed, and Charlie never missed an opportunity to talk, but I knew better. James was doing this on purpose. I glanced over at him, and I swear I saw him smirking. *This man is impossible!*

Given the circumstances, I motioned for Charlie to start.

He selected the first option. Charlie was a free spirit; he loved everything to be fun and colorful. He selected our most casual proposal.

When he was done, James nodded. Then he turned his gaze on me. "Ms. Mills?"

Damn him and that sultry tone of his! I drank some water so I could salivate a little, and then I began. "I am proud of each of these proposals. However, if I had to select only one, I would have to say it would be this proposal." I pointed toward our last board. "This was the last idea pitched, but it is by far my personal favorite. The colors and the illustrations automatically attract the male population. However, the different tones of the colors allow for the brand to appear warm and cozy, and that invites the female population. Although the vast majority of whiskey drinkers are males, there is a large percentage of what are known as 'whiskey girls.' This proposal focuses on the classic down-home feeling that most people are looking for when they go have a drink."

The room was silent. I wasn't sure if that was a good or bad thing. I looked around, and the team was wide-eyed, while Christopher, Blake, and James just stared at me.

Why on earth do I feel like I am on trial? Did I say something wrong? As I stood there, I remembered my Superman pose, so I mentally did that until someone said something.

Finally, Blake took the lead. "Well said, my dear."

Christopher nodded, and James just stared a hole in me.

I saw Blake elbow James, and he snapped out of whatever was happening. "Mr. Lewis, Ms. Mills, thank you for your insight into these proposals. I am truly impressed. When I began producing my line of whiskey, I had a vision. I didn't know how to put it into words or visuals, but you all have taken my thoughts and have developed a great campaign. After carefully considering all three proposals, I must say that Ms. Mills has sold me on the third proposal."

I was shocked that he chose mine. Charlie spun his idea with such ease. He made it sound enjoyable. I didn't feel half as confident as he was.

Ana must have caught on to my distress because she then took the floor. "Mr. Still, I am pleased to know that my team has assembled a proposal that meets your standards. I am positive that they will continue the great work throughout the progression of this campaign. Now, as I understand it, we are well past our allotted time, and Mr. Gary and Mr. Wilks have another meeting in less than fifteen minutes. Thank you for your time, gentlemen!"

Christopher, Blake, and James all nodded and departed.

Chapter 6

Okay, so I might have gone off script when I presented my favorite proposal. To be honest, my favorite was the one Charlie presented, but I couldn't very well present the same thing. We had to pitch an alternative. I think everyone was wide-eyed and speechless because they knew that was not my favorite. I have no idea what came over me and why I pitched it the way I did, but I'm glad I did. Now we have to move forward with this campaign, and I'm hoping someone else on the team feels the way I did.

Landon came into my office. "Christy, Mr. Stevens is on the line. He would like to discuss some changes his company would like to make to his campaign."

I nodded and had Landon put him through to my line. "Mr. Stevens! Good morning, how are you doing today?"

We remained on a phone conference for the majority of the morning. He had quite a few things going on, and he wanted to make sure everything came out at the same time as his new vodka line. Right before noon, Annie sent me a text asking if I wanted to go to De Mayo's. I typed a quick reply and finished up my conference with Mr. Stevens.

I made my way downstairs. I decided to take the stairs since I was heading across the street to stuff my face. At least, this way, I wouldn't feel so bad. I met up with Annie, and we sat at our favorite booth at the back of the restaurant. Annie and I were both people watchers, and sitting in this booth allowed us to see who came in and out of the place.

"Ladies, lunch is served! Enjoy!" Linda was our waitress at De Mayo's. She always had our order put in before we could get to our seat.

"Thanks, Linda!" we said in unison.

Annie and I were talking about our weekend plans when I felt someone watching me. I turned my head while Annie was suggesting we go back to Miami to help Lilly pack some stuff up and ship it back this way. When I looked over my shoulder, I saw Christopher and Blake sitting at a high-top with none other than James Still. Christopher and Blake were talking, but James was looking directly at me.

Annie leaned over to see what I was looking at, and she let out a loud laugh.

That caught my attention. I snapped my head back around. "Annie!!!" I loudly whispered.

She shook her head and covered her mouth. "I'm sorry, Christy! It's just that…what are the odds?! This is just too much."

I shook my head. *This is ridiculous! Will I ever get a chance to just breathe?! I know he saw me, but I really hope he doesn't make his way over here because I would much rather enjoy my Mayo burger.*

Annie stuck a fry out at me, so I bit it. She gaped at me.

I heard a deep laugh behind me. I closed my eyes for a second before I reacted. I slowly turned around and found James standing there. He had a boyish grin on his face, and it did me in. I couldn't be upset that he appeared everywhere I went.

"Ms. Meyers, Ms. Mills, I won't take too much of your time. Ms. Mills, I wonder if you could take some time out of your busy schedule to join me for dinner tonight. I would like to discuss some things with you."

I smiled at him because I knew exactly where he was going with this. It had been three weeks since he had said we had to talk about what happened in Miami, and then he had caught me in a similar situation this weekend.

I think he knew what I was thinking because he simply nodded and said, "All right then. I shall send a car to pick you up at 7:00 p.m. Enjoy the rest of your meal, ladies." He excused himself and walked away.

I turned back to see Annie watching me intently. "What the hell was that?"

I laughed. "Not sure what you mean, sweets."

She scowled at me. "You know exactly what I mean. When did you two develop a secret language?! I never heard you say yes, nor did I see you nod your head."

I laughed and bit my burger. After I swallowed the food in my mouth, I reminded Annie of the promise that he made in Miami.

She thought back and then remembered that it happened then and again this past weekend.

We finished our food and made our way back to work. The afternoon went by pretty fast, given all of the meetings

I had to hold due to the adjustments Mr. Stevens was requesting. When 5:30 p.m. came around, I rode the elevator down and met Annie in the lobby.

"Hey, lady! You ready to get home?"

Oh Lord! She was scheming all afternoon; I know it! "Annie, please tell me that you have not been planning all afternoon?"

She let out a loud laugh as she hailed a cab for us.

Traffic wasn't too bad. We made it to our place by 5:50 p.m. I jumped in the shower as soon as I got home. Although I knew nothing was going to happen tonight, I shaved. When I got out of the shower, Annie had already set out an outfit for me and was waiting to do my hair and makeup. I'm glad I shaved because the dress this kid picked out was revealing in all the wrong, but right, places. I narrowed my eyes at her.

She laughed and pulled me into the chair. "Oh hush, Christy! You know that man wants you, so why not take advantage of that fact!"

This girl is impossible!

As 7:00 p.m. neared, I heard a knock at the door. I looked up at Annie.

She said, "Just in time! I'm all done! Go have some fun, and don't do anything I wouldn't do!"

I made my way down the hall and opened the door. There he was, standing in a three-piece suit and looking incredible! He looked me over from head to toe, and when our eyes met, I saw his jaw snap and the vein in his neck throb very fast.

"Don't like what you see, Mr. Still?" I twirled a strand of hair around my index finger and feigned innocence.

His eyes narrowed. "Quite the contrary, Ms. Mills. Shall we head to dinner?"

I loved that I had this effect on him. I waved to Annie and closed the door behind me. As we walked out to the car, I felt James's hand on the small of my back. I had a feeling I needed to get used to that this evening; he was not going to take his hands off me because someone might misunderstand and think I was available.

We reached the car, and his driver opened the door. "Good evening, Ms. Mills."

I smiled, and James took my hand to help me into the car. He gave directions to his driver, and then he got in next to me. I had scooched all the way to the other side of the car, and he purposely sat very close to me, but was careful not to touch me. I could feel the warmth from his body, and the intensity of his stare was giving me chills.

I turned to look at James, and his stare was mesmerizing. His expression softened, and I wasn't sure what to make of it. We stared at each other in silence for the short ride to the restaurant. When the car came to a stop, he stepped out of the vehicle and reached for my hand. I took it so he could help me out of the car.

We walked into the restaurant, and the hostess said she had our table ready. She escorted us to a secluded area in the back of the restaurant. It was a little nook hidden from the rowdiness of the other guests. James pulled my chair out, and then he took the chair across from me.

"How was your day, Ms. Mills?"

Although I loved that he was so respectful, I wasn't sure I wanted him to call me Ms. Mills all the time. I almost said something, but I thought better of it and just answered his question.

"My day was quite eventful. My team and I had a series of meetings to address the changes that were needed for the other campaigns that we are managing. How was your day?"

He took a while to think, as if the question were very difficult. "My day was slow-moving until I ran into you at lunch."

That was an interesting thing to say. I think he said it so he could monitor my expressions. I tried to put my poker face so I wouldn't give anything away. "Oh? Do tell."

He looked at me, and I knew he was catching on to me. "Ms. Mills, a day that involves you is never a normal day."

Just then, the waitress walked up and asked if she could take our drink order. She was transfixed by James. Not once did she look my way. Not even when James asked what kind of wine I was interested in drinking.

This is going to be a fun evening. I don't want to be petty, so I am going to play this the innocent way. "I am sure any wine you select, Mr. Still, will be suitable for the evening."

He must have heard the playfulness in my tone because he gave me a devilish grin and ordered a Malbec. The waitress kept coming back to flirt with him. It was a bit annoying that she thought it appropriate, but I made sure not to give anything away. She came back for our order and, of course, first asked James what he wanted.

He deferred to me. "What will you be having, Ms. Mills?" As the waitress turned to look at me, he winked at me.

I wanted to laugh, but I had to keep it together. "I will have an eight-ounce, medium-rare steak with mashed potatoes and asparagus."

She wrote it down and then turned to James with a smile. "And for you, sir?"

He ordered a steak as well. As she walked away, James turned to me, "Care to tell me what game you are playing?"

I giggled. "Whatever do you mean, Mr. Still?"

He shook his head. "Have it your way then."

I took a sip of wine and turned on my professional side. "Tell me, Mr. Still, why have you brought me here tonight?" I could tell he was taken aback by my tone, but he did not change his facial expression.

"Ms. Mills, I am sure it can be of no surprise why I have invited you to dine with me tonight. A few weeks ago, we ran into each other and said we were going to discuss said encounter when we got back into town. Needless to say, it has been rather busy, and we have not yet gotten a chance to discuss it, but then it happened again. The initial encounter had you in a bit of a rage, while the second was welcomed…if I deduced correctly."

He took a sip of wine. I believe it was to give me a minute to reflect and react.

I, too, sipped my wine, and when I set the glass down, I felt a bit of nervous courage. I bit my lip and then proceeded to respond, "Mr. Still, I was indeed outraged by your actions a few weeks ago. I was caught off guard, in an entirely different city, while I was under the influence. I am sure, if the roles were reversed, you might not have reacted any differently. Now, as for the second encounter, yes, you were correct to deduce that I was pleased that you were there to intervene. Had it not been for you, that night might have ended up a horrible cliché about a drunk girl and an overzealous guy."

I could see the vein in his jaw working. *I really need to figure out what his triggers are because this is not a good sign.*

"Nonetheless, I appreciate your interference on both occasions."

The waitress brought our food, and he snapped out of whatever mood and thoughts were running through his mind. He looked up at her and said thank you. He waited until she disappeared before he looked back at me.

"Tell me... Why did you approach me that night at the bar when we first met?"

Oh, great. Here we go. I was wondering when our conversation was going to circle back to THAT night. What the hell am I supposed to say? "I thought you were hot and wanted to take you home?"

I took a drink of my wine and sat back in the chair. "Is it really necessary to discuss a point in our lives when we were complete strangers?"

I don't think he was expecting that response because he looked a little bemused. He blinked before he responded, "I happen to believe that it is extremely necessary to discuss that night. I would like to know what was running through your mind when you decided to approach me that night."

His tone led me to believe that he was not going to take no for an answer. I dropped the professional card because—let's face it—this was by no means work related. "If you must know, the night I saw you in the bar, I was thinking that you were extremely hot, and I wanted to flirt with you a bit to see if maybe I could take you home with me. That is not something I normally do, but I had a pretty bad week, and I needed something to get my mind off everything. I mistakenly thought going that route was a good idea. I had never attempted such a thing, and now know I will never attempt it again."

I believed the wine was getting the best of me, so I cut a piece of steak and began eating because, at this rate, I would be wasted before I ate anything. I could see that James didn't know how to respond to what I had just said because he just watched me cut my food and eat a few pieces of steak.

I hope that he doesn't ask me why I was having a bad week because I really am not in the mood to deal with all that mess right now.

James ate a bit as he watched me intently. Then, when he had composed himself, I assume, he proceeded to respond, "Christy"—his tone was soft, almost as if talking to a child—"I hope that you don't think I did not feel the same about you. The moment I saw you when you walked into the bar, I was in awe of you, but I was in a bad place myself. When you came up to me, I was hoping that I would turn you off by my pessimism so that I wouldn't have to actually interact with you. I was afraid that if I interacted with you, I wouldn't be able to stop. Now, that point has been proven. I can't keep away from you…even if I wanted to. You have bewitched me, and no matter how hard you try to deny it, I know that you feel the same."

I nearly choked on a piece of meat. *Damn, this guy is good! How can he make me feel better about one of the worst situations in my life?*

He reached across the table—to where my hand was lying by my wineglass—and he picked up my hand. "Honey, don't do that." I looked up at James, and he continued, "Don't be ashamed of what you just told me. I am fascinated by your ability to have that kind of courage. The kind of courage that I didn't have that night." He rubbed his thumb on the back of my hand. I wasn't sure what he was getting at, but we discussed the situation a little more, and James made me feel better about it.

When we finished dinner, he asked if I wanted dessert. Of course, my dirty mind went straight to the gutter. I think he caught on because he laughed and kindly declined the waitress's offer of dessert and asked for the check.

After dinner, we took a walk. The night was cool and pleasant. Discussing the night we met had cleared the air between James and me, and I felt more comfortable around him. I felt that James, too, was more relaxed around me. As we were walking, he actually put an arm around me and pulled me close to him. We walked like that for a few blocks.

We came up to an apartment complex with a doorman, and James pulled me toward the door. I looked up at him and stopped walking.

"Where are we going?"

He gave me my favorite boyish grin of his. "This is my apartment complex. I thought we could have a nightcap here and maybe have the dessert you have been wanting." He winked at me, and I felt myself blush. He gently pulled me closer, and I followed him.

We rode the elevator all the way to the top.

Of course, it's a penthouse.

He must have seen the questions in my eyes because he laughed a little. "This is my place in the city. When I am doing business, this is where I stay. Excuse the mess. I don't host anyone here."

When we entered the penthouse, I looked around. I wasn't sure what mess he was talking about. There were a lot of warm colors in his apartment. Large furnishings, but very warm and cozy. I walked over to the couch and took a seat toward one of the ends.

James excused himself to get us some wine. When he came back, I was sitting and staring at a painting that was hanging directly across from me. He sat next to me and handed me a glass.

"It's an interesting piece of art, is it not?" His voice brought me out of my head.

"It is breathtaking! I didn't realize you were an art connoisseur."

He laughed and draped an arm over the couch behind me. "There are many things you do not know about me, Christy Mills, but I hope to change that soon."

I laughed. "Do you tell that to all the girls you bring here?"

He stiffened, put his wineglass down on the coffee table, and grabbed my chin to turn my head so that I faced him. "I do not bring any women to my home. You would be the first female to enter this apartment."

I was so shocked by his reaction that I couldn't respond. I simply nodded.

He was still holding my chin as he said, "Good," and leaned in to kiss me.

It was a warm kiss with a bit of seduction. I was caught off guard by it, but it felt amazing. He coaxed my mouth open, and his tongue made its way into my mouth. I gave in to his kiss and put my arms around his neck. Things began to get heated when the kiss got deeper.

I was wearing practically nothing, but the little dress I did have on didn't give too easily. However, that didn't stop James from pulling me onto his lap. My dress rode up as I straddled him. He wrapped his arms around me, and let his hands roam everywhere.

I was sure this was probably going to bite me in the ass later, but I didn't care. There was too much tension between us that needed to be released. It was as if we were two teenagers having a hot make-out session because we were both still fully clothed. But I was ready as ever, and I know he was ready because he was hard as a rock underneath me.

James pulled away from me a bit to examine my face. Whatever it was he was looking for, I assume he got confirmation because he picked me up and began walking down the hall until we reached a door that was closed. He held me against the door so he could open it, and then he walked into a moonlit room. There was a giant bed in the center of the room. I could only imagine that this was the master bedroom.

He set me down on the edge of the bed and stood between my legs. The way he looked at me took my breath away. He shimmied my dress up my hips and then pulled it over my head. Annie had made me wear red lingerie underneath my—literally—little black dress. When James set eyes on my skimpy red bra and panties, his expression grew dark. His eyes were heavy with lust. He leaned in to kiss me and gently pushed me back onto the bed. When he was certain I was lying down, he began kissing me deeper. I let my hands roam as I unbuttoned James's black dress shirt as he trailed kisses down my jaw and neck.

"Christy, you looked incredible tonight, but right now you look absolutely breathtaking."

That made me feel all warm inside. He continued kissing me as I finished working on the buttons of his shirt. He helped me pull it off him.

My God, he is absolutely gorgeous! James was defined in all the areas that mattered, but he wasn't over-the-top like most gym rats.

He trailed kisses from my neck to my cleavage. Meanwhile, his hands played with my breasts. He was simultaneously rolling both my nipples in his fingers, and if he kept doing that, I might just come immediately. As if reading my mind, he slowed his rhythm and unclasped my bra. He pulled it off and admired the girls for a minute.

"Is there no part of you that isn't perfect?"

He cupped my boobs, and they fit perfectly in his hands. He played with the nipples to make them taut again, and then he took one of them into his mouth. His hands never stopped. He was caressing my leg from the outside and then made his way back up my leg on the inside. This gave me chills. It was so sensual I almost couldn't bear it! When he reached my thigh he made circular motions as he rolled my nipple in his mouth. It was absolutely erotic. He popped the nipple out of his mouth and moved on to the other breast. When he began rolling that nipple around in his mouth, his hand made it to my clit. His thumb rolled my clit at the same tempo as his tongue rolled my nipple. It was so sensual I was close to climaxing.

"Honey, you are so wet for me."

My body must have warned James because he moved his hand farther into my folds and pushed a finger into me. As he slid it in and out, he raised his head to kiss me. He bit my lip at the same time he inserted another finger.

"Christy, you are so tight! I can't wait to get inside of you."

I moaned, "Then don't."

He bit me again. "Honey, I have to prep you because I don't want to hurt you, but don't worry. I will be inside you soon enough."

As he was thrusting two fingers inside of me, he was also circling my clit with his thumb. That pushed me over the edge. I screamed as I came. James kissed me deeply as I finished climaxing. Then he pulled away, put his fingers in his mouth, and licked my juices.

"You taste delicious." He winked at me. "Don't move."

He took off his pants and did a low-key striptease. Propped up on my elbows, I giggled and watched. When he was done, he came back toward me and pulled my panties off me. He tossed them somewhere and started kissing my navel. He trailed down and ended up in between my legs. He blew warm air over my skin, and it was delectable. Then he began licking. His tongue was incredible, and the things he could do with it were amazing! I didn't last long before I climaxed again, and he licked me the entire time, until I was done.

"How do you feel, honey?"

Eyes heavy, I looked up at James and gave him a smile. "I feel amazing!"

He growled a little triumphantly. "I am glad you feel that way, but we haven't even gotten started." He reached for a condom and put it on himself. He pushed me up farther on the bed and then kissed me. It was gentle, the kind of kiss a boy gives a girl on their first date.

When he spread my legs, he deepened the kiss. His tongue pushed against mine, and he slowly started pushing inside of me. He was incredibly thick. He had only inserted the tip of his cock, and my pussy was taking its time adjusting to his size. It was painful, but in a good way. He pushed in very slowly, and it was amazing. It took a little time for him to get all the way in, but when he did, it was a perfect fit.

"Are you all right, honey? I don't want to hurt you. Tell me if it hurts, okay?"

I licked my lips and nodded. "It hurts so good. Keep going."

He kissed my nose and began thrusting in and out of me in a slow motion. We established a rhythm together, and I could feel the nerve bundles starting to kick. James began moving faster, and he used his thumb to rub my clit, all while sucking on my nipple.

My body couldn't take the sensations. "I'm almost there, James."

He moved the hair out of my face, kissed me, and said, "Me too, honey! Stay with me, okay?"

We moved a little faster, and both of us came in a rush. I saw stars! It was euphoric! He slowed his thrusts until we were both spent. Then, he lay still on top of me, and I wrapped my arms around him. He was still semi-erect inside of me. I am sure I was losing my mind, but I wanted to go again. He peppered me with soft kisses as he lay on top of me, and I ran my fingernails up and down his back. It was perfect.

We lay there for a little while. I rubbed his back until I heard a light snore escape from his mouth. I didn't have the desire to move. He was still inside of me, and there wasn't anywhere else I would rather be. I lay there listening to him for some time until eventually I fell asleep.

***

I was so warm, and for a moment I thought I was lying out in the sun somewhere. The sun gleamed lightly on my face, and then I felt a pleasurable pain and remembered where I was. I licked my lips and turned my head to find James staring intently at me with a mischievous look on his face. Then I felt the pain again. He was pushing in and out of me, and it felt amazing. I was extremely sore from last night, but this was not the least bit uncomfortable. He pushed in a little more forcefully, and I let out a moan. He bit my lip and then soothed it with his tongue. We kissed deeply while he moved in and out of me. It was nice and slow for a little while, until I began to feel the climax coming.

James sped up. "Stay with me, honey. I'm close too." He kissed my neck and began running his hands down my body. He rubbed my breasts until my nipples were taut. He swiped his tongue across them a few times while his hand moved down between us. His thumb circled my clit, and I couldn't hold it in anymore.

"James, I'm so close! Don't stop!"

He sucked on my nipple and continued his slow movements over my clit while his thrusts became faster and rougher. I screamed, and we came together. He slowed his thrusts and kissed my neck until I stopped shaking from the climax.

I licked my lips and looked up at this gorgeous man. "Well, good morning to you too."

James laughed and kissed me.

Chapter 7

James got up and walked toward the bathroom. I heard the shower turn on and then saw him walk back toward me with a washcloth in his hand. He crawled on the bed and caressed my legs while pulling them apart. He wiped me clean and returned to the bathroom.

I don't think anyone has ever cleaned me up after sex. I'm not sure if this is awkward or not. What am I supposed to do now while he showers? I lay in bed, fearful that moving would make things more awkward. *Maybe once James jumps in the shower, I'll get dressed and leave him a note.*

He may have sensed I was about to flee. He appeared in the doorway, leaned against the doorframe, and crossed his arms. "God, you look beautiful in the morning."

I burst into giggles. I knew he was lying because I was certain I looked hideous in the morning.

James took that as an invitation and walked toward me. He grabbed one of my legs and pulled me toward the end of the bed. He leaned down, pressed a kiss on my nose, and then picked me up and carried me toward the bathroom.

I wrapped my arms around his neck and leaned my head against his chest as we walked to the bathroom. It was strange how safe I felt in his arms. I don't think I had ever felt like that before. When we got into the bathroom, I picked up my head and saw that it was very spacious, and the shower was incredible! It had a waterfall effect, and I immediately longed to stand underneath it.

We headed for the shower; James opened the door and walked us inside. The water felt amazing on my skin. He set me down gently underneath the waterfall. I tilted my head back and let the water run down my body. I ran my hands through my hair and just enjoyed the moment.

Then I felt James get closer to me. He pinned me to the wall and kissed me. He trailed kisses down my neck, my chest, to my navel. The next thing I knew, he was on his knees, lifting me up and placing my legs on his shoulders. He blew lightly on my sensitive flesh and then began licking at my folds. At first, it was light and gentle; then he went deeper and faster. My God, was his tongue amazing. He moved from my inner folds to my clit. He swiped at it and then sucked it into his mouth as I moaned and shivered. He stuck a finger inside me and moved slowly. He played with my clit for a little bit, and then he stuck another finger inside of me and sucked on my clit at the same time. It was incredible, and I began to climax again. He worked his magic, and I was shaking with the intensity of my orgasm.

He held on to me until I stopped shaking. Then, he set me down gently and licked his fingers. He stood up and said, "I have been wanting to do that since the night I saw you at the bar. You taste amazing, sweetheart. I am afraid you might be addicting."

I was still spent from that climax, so James leaned in, kissed me, and then turned me around. He washed my entire body and rinsed me off while I was still practically limp. *Is this guy for real? I mean…damn!* I don't think I have ever had mind-blowing sex and then been bathed right after.

As James was rinsing me off, I regained a semblance of strength. I turned back around and reached for his body wash. I washed him down and let him rinse off. When he turned off the water, he reached out and handed me a towel and then grabbed one for himself.

Once we were dry, we walked back to the bedroom. Since I didn't have any clean clothing and wasn't planning on putting on the dress from last night, I was in a bit of a pickle. I walked toward the bed and sat down while he walked toward the closet. He came back wearing pajama bottoms; he had a T-shirt in his hand.

He walked up to me and said, "Lift your arms." After I did as I was told, he pulled the T-shirt over my head and took my towel. The shirt was warm and cozy and smelled exactly like him.

"Ready for some breakfast?"

I wasn't sure what the deal was, but why not go along with it? "Sure."

James held out his hand, and I placed mine in his. He gave me a light pull, and I jumped off the bed. We walked out of the bedroom, through the living room, and into a back room. The kitchen was incredible! It was spacious and uniquely designed to match him. He let go of my hand and asked if I wanted coffee.

I nodded my head. While I waited, I looked around the room, admired the furnishings, and landed on the view from the bay window. It was incredible.

He wrapped an arm around me, kissed my cheek, and handed me a cup of coffee. "There is cream and sugar on the island if you care for some." He walked away and started pulling items out of the fridge.

I turned back to admire the view for another minute before I made my way to the island to prepare my coffee. The coffee was delicious, and the view was incredible. James looked mouthwatering as he made his way around the kitchen. I walked around the island and leaned against it watching him. He was agile and looked comfortable. I never imagined he would be a cook. Then again, I really wasn't sure what I imagined. I took another sip of coffee, and he turned around to find me ogling him.

He gave a half grin. "Like what you see?"

I giggled. "As a matter of fact, I do."

He pulled out some plates and set the eggs and bacon on them before walking toward me. He put his arms on either side of me and caged me in against the island. He bit my lip and then kissed me deeply. I looped my arms around his neck, and he wrapped his arms around my waist. It was extremely hot, but he broke it off before things got heated.

"Breakfast will get cold." He gave me one last kiss and then handed me a plate. He took a seat at the island, and

I stood across from him. "Don't like to sit down when you eat?"

I shook my head. "Not in the mornings. Annie and I always eat standing up. We have had this habit since college."

He nodded his head and took a sip of his coffee. "You ladies seem to have a strong friendship. How long have you all been friends?"

I didn't realize how hungry I was until I set my fork down and realized I was done with my food. I set my plate in the sink, and I looked up at him. He was watching me intently. The way his eyes followed me made me get goose bumps.

"We met freshman year of college. And have been best friends since. We have been through a lot together, and that has led us to build a solid friendship. I wasn't blessed with a sister by birth, but she has become my sister."

I noticed he had finished his food, so I picked up his plate and began washing the dishes. I had OCD about leaving dirty dishes lying around.

"Leave them in the sink. The housekeeper will get to them later."

I shook my head and was done washing them before he was able to get up and walk around the island. He set his coffee mug down, and I washed that as well. I dried my hands and turned to find him staring at me again. I leaned against the island and stared back. I licked my lips and bit my bottom lip, a bad habit I picked up years ago.

James's eyes grew dark, and he walked toward me. Much like earlier, he caged me in with his hands on either side of me. He bit at the loose part of my lip and worked his way over to free the other side. Then he began kissing me softly but firmly as I placed my hands on his chest and felt the strength of his muscles underneath my hands. He wrapped his arms around my waist and lifted me onto the island.

It was cold on my ass, but the contrast between the cold stone and the warmth of his body gave me a rush. I wrapped my legs around his waist and immediately felt his dick, which was hard and ready. It made me wet just knowing the effect I had on him. I reached between us and put my hand down his pajama bottoms. As I suspected, he wasn't wearing any underwear. I wrapped my hand around his thick, straining dick and began working my way up and down it. I started slowly, but began moving faster when I heard a light moan escape his lips.

I pulled his dick out of his bottoms and bent down to swipe the tip with my tongue. He tasted sweet, and I wanted to taste more of him, but I think my tongue pushed him over the edge. He pulled my head up and my waist to the edge of the island top; then he thrust inside of me.

"Honey, I love that you are so ready for me. You look incredibly gorgeous in the morning, and you wearing nothing but my T-shirt is not helping. Are you with me? Because I am not going to last."

Given that we had already had satisfying orgasms twice this morning, this was considered a quickie. I don't think either of us could really last too long. We moved in a fast rhythm and came fairly quickly. He grabbed the hand towel that he had tossed me earlier and spread my legs. He wiped me clean, wiped himself, and then tossed the towel in the sink. He lifted me up and walked me into the living room.

The strength and the stamina of this guy are incredible. I wonder how many times a week he works out? I'm not extremely heavy, but I'm also not light as a feather.

He set me down on a blanket on the couch. "Want to watch a movie?" James asked me as if it was the most normal of Saturdays for him. It was crazy how comfortable he was acting.

It appeared I was the only one having internal panic attacks. I couldn't speak, so I just nodded.

He walked over to the entertainment center, grabbed some remote controls, and walked back to the couch. Instead of sitting next to me, he sat on the other end of the couch.

How strange is that? I didn't say anything.

He turned on the TV and asked, "Do you have a preference?"

I wasn't sure what I felt like watching, so I went with, "No, I like the majority of genres. Pick something you like." It wasn't a lie. I really did like all movie types, but I half wanted to see what his interests were.

He scrolled down a list and finally settled on an action movie. Before he hit Play, he asked if I wanted a snack or anything to drink.

I shook my head and turned to watch the movie as he hit Play.

Before the movie got started, though, he pressed some buttons on another remote control, and some window coverings came down from the ceiling, turning the room dark and movie-appropriate. It suddenly became cooler, so I covered myself with the blanket that was underneath me.

The previews played, and the movie began. He sat still with his legs on the coffee table. Instead of watching the movie, I was intent on watching James. He was as still as a statue, but relaxed. It looked as if he didn't have a care in the world. I couldn't picture a guy like him having many Saturdays like this.

Eventually, I stopped staring at him, for fear of looking crazy. I began watching the movie, and it was pretty cool. About halfway through the movie, I started getting sleepy, but I couldn't get comfortable. I had attempted to wiggle around silently, so I would not disturb him, but I still couldn't get comfy. I know he had sat on the other side of the couch for a reason, but I really didn't care. I crawled over and snuggled up to his side. I thought I was going to freak him out, but he pulled me closer and wrapped the blanket around us.

A loud crash woke me. I opened my eyes and saw it was just the movie. I looked up to see James had dozed off too. He had his arm wrapped around me and his head tilted back on the back of the couch. He looked beautiful when he slept. I looked him over and then noticed his pajama bottoms tenting.

My goodness, does this man ever stop thinking about sex? Even in his sleep he is ready to go.

I couldn't help myself. I carefully moved his bottoms and popped out his dick. It was crazy how fully erect he was. I looked up and saw he was still sleeping. His arm had slipped down to my waist which gave me perfect access and the ability to move. I slowly bent over and placed my lips around his cock. I sucked him in and out nice and slow. I watched him so I could see what his reaction was, but he hadn't woken up yet. I swiped my tongue over the tip a few times, and then I heard a moan escape his lips. He began moving a little, and then I saw his eyes open.

He smiled sleepily at me and moved his hand from my waist to my neck. He moved my hair out of the way and then leaned his head back. I kept a slow pace for a little while, and when I got a taste of his pre-cum, I started sucking faster. I could feel him tighten, and I knew he was close. He started moaning more, and his hand gripped my hair a little tighter. I opened my mouth a little wider and took him all the way to the back of my throat. That pushed him over the edge. He came, and I could feel it running down my throat, nice and warm. I drank it all and slowed my sucking until he was spent. He let go of my hair, and I kissed the tip of his dick.

Then James pulled me up and kissed me. "That was incredible!"

I kissed him back and snuggled next to him.

Some other movie had come on, and we began watching that. We both ended up falling asleep again. I got the urge to go to the bathroom, and when I opened my eyes, the credits were rolling on that movie. I looked up to see James was still sleeping. I wiggled my way out of his embrace, making sure I didn't wake him, and made my way to the bathroom. I did my business, and when I went to wash my hands, I saw my reflection.

He must be crazy! He called me gorgeous and beautiful twice, and my hair is crazy-sex hair!

I ran my wet fingers through it and tried to fix it. Once I was semi-satisfied with what I saw, I made my way back to the living room. He was still sleeping. I couldn't get over the fact that he looked so gorgeous when he slept. I made my way back to the couch, and since I didn't want to wake him, I lay on the other end of the couch. I watched the TV mindlessly and fell asleep again.

I'm not certain how long I slept, but I woke up when I felt a pair of lips kissing the inside of my thighs. He was blowing lightly and following up with gentle kisses that led to their apex. He rubbed his index finger up and down my clit. I felt drunk because all I could do was lie there; it was so pleasurable. He spread my labia and inserted his index finger, pushing in and out until it slid easily. Then he added his middle finger and pushed both inside of me.

Slowly, he moved in and out of me, and the way my pussy widened felt incredible.

He then added his thumb to the mix. While he pushed both fingers inside of me, his thumb circled my clitoris. How he managed to do that was beyond me, but it felt wonderful. He did that for a little bit before he removed his thumb and replaced it with his tongue. He swiped up and down. He removed his fingers momentarily to lick my juices off them and to stick his tongue inside of me. I moaned with delight. He licked inside of me and then moved to my clit. When he got to my clit, he reinserted both fingers and began moving rapidly. The combination made me absolutely euphoric. I was in so much pleasure that I began seeing stars and shaking until my body climaxed. He removed his fingers and licked all of my juices until I stopped shaking and my body went limp.

I must have fallen asleep because, when I came to, I was alone in the living room. The window coverings were slightly lifted, and I could see the sun shining brightly.

Holy shit! What time is it? Where is my phone?! Annie is going to kill me!! We were supposed to scope out houses for Lilly and Aiden today!

I found my purse on the entrance table. I rummaged through it and found my phone. *Fuck!* I had thirty messages and ten missed calls! I walked back to the couch and began looking through my missed calls. Annie called me five times, Michael called me twice, Lilly called me twice, and Luke called me once. I began reading the texts.

The majority were from Annie, of course. A lot of *where are you* and *you better call me ASAP* texts. Michael also sent me a few.

Man oh man, they are going to kill me if I don't start calling them back. I walked toward the kitchen and dialed Annie. It rang a few times before I heard her pick up.

"Christy Mills! WHERE THE HELL HAVE YOU BEEN?!?!"

I let her speak her peace before I responded, "Sweets, relax. I am okay! Everything is fine. I'm fine. I'm sorry I messed up our plans for today, but I promise we shall go house hunting this week after work, yeah?"

She went on about how irresponsible I was, and I let her go on like that until she talked herself out of it. She asked if I would be home later, and I said I'd let her know. We finished our conversation, and I was about to dial Michael when I felt warmth radiating from behind me.

I was about to turn around, but James wrapped his arms around me and kissed my neck. "Care to tell me who you will be house hunting with?"

Did he seriously eavesdrop on me? What the hell, and why on earth is he asking about my business? "Eavesdropping is very rude, Mr. Still."

He laughed and kissed me once more right below my ear. "You are quite right about that, Ms. Mills, but it is not considered eavesdropping when you are having a conversation in public."

He had a good point. I was just standing in the middle of his kitchen, having a conversation. "Regardless of public or private conversations, unless they are addressed to you, you shouldn't inquire about them."

He gave me a squeeze and took a step back. "Honey, what's with the attitude? I was just making conversation. You don't need to let me in if you don't want to."

Great, Christy! Why do you have to have so many damn trust issues!? Now, he probably thinks you're crazy! Ugh, I really need to get it together when it comes to James.

I turned to face him. He was leaning against the island with his hands on the island. I set my phone on the table and walked over to him. I wrapped my arms around him and kissed his neck.

"Hey, I am sorry. As you may have noticed, I am not good at having people in my personal business, but I'm working on it."

He wrapped his arms around me then, gave me a squeeze, and kissed the top of my head. "Want some lunch?"

I looked up and nodded at him.

He gave me a swift kiss and walked away. He called back, "Takeout okay?"

I put my finger to my chin and pretended to think. "Sure, that works."

He laughed and went into the other room to get the phone and order.

In the meantime, I called Mike. He was livid that I hadn't had the decency to notify him or Annie that I wouldn't be coming home. They apparently had all gone out last night and were expecting me to meet up with them. I apologized to him and told him I wouldn't do it again. Mike and I had been through a lot, and when we went missing for longer than a few hours, we always thought the worst. We talked a little more about the next weekend and how everyone wanted to get together and go out to the lake.

As always, I was already thinking of making excuses, but before I could get a word in, Mike told me to shut it and that we would revisit the topic later in the week. He knew being out on the lake was not my first choice, but I was always overruled. Everyone else loved to fish and water ski, so I already knew what my plans were going to be next weekend.

We were finishing up our conversation when he said, "Oh, by the way, Luke was asking about you last night. He wanted to know where you were. Don't think he's ever asked that. Talk to ya later!"

I stared at the phone wide-mouthed for a second. *I cannot believe he did that!* I meant to return Luke's call, but I thought better of it. *It's a conversation best had at home. The problem is I am so comfortable here. I have been walking around half naked in the presence of a gorgeous man, and I haven't had a single panic attack. I am not certain that I am ready to go home. I don't even know what James and I are doing.*

As if sensing my anxiety, James walked into the kitchen. "Everything all right? You look a little pale."

I snapped out of it quickly. "Yes, thanks for asking. My friends were just worried as to why I didn't come home and were wondering if I was all right. What's for lunch?"

He thought about what I said and for a second it looked as if he was going to counter with an "I don't believe you," but he didn't. Instead, he answered, "Chinese."

We had lunch in the living room; the TV was on, and both of us watched it mindlessly. I couldn't help thinking about everything that was going on. I wondered what Mike would think about this situation. I was almost certain he would say, "I can't believe you're still making these senseless decisions," or something like that. *I have a feeling that Mike is going to let me have it next time we see each other. I'm over here, sleeping with James—which, mind you, is a decision that I could have made differently. I'm not sure what the consequences of this decision will be, but I really hope it doesn't come back to bite me in the ass.*

I had feelings for James, but they were small and contained. But after last night and this morning, they have grown a lot. He is sweet, caring, and passionate—not to mention extremely handsome.

"Christy? Christy."

I snapped out of my daydream and turned to look at James. "I'm sorry. What did you say?"

His eyes narrowed. "Are you all right?"

I smiled at him. "Yes, I'm fine. What were you asking me?"

He gave me a look I couldn't read. "I was wondering if there was something wrong with your lunch?"

I looked down at my plate and realized I hadn't eaten much. "No, there is nothing wrong with it. To be honest, I was daydreaming."

He tilted his head. "Penny for your thoughts?"

I smiled at him and said, "Nothing important going on in there."

He gave me that look again, the one that I had begun classifying as his "I don't believe you" face. I looked at him for a little bit and realized I was doing it again. He had gotten up and was now sitting on the couch.

I stood up, walked over to him, and sat on his lap. He pulled me close, and I laid my head on his chest. "I was thinking about how much I like the bubble we've been living in and how great you are."

He ran his hand up and down my leg slowly. "Bubble?"

I laughed. "Yes, bubble. It has been ages since I have gone completely off-grid for longer than an hour. I imagine it's the same for you."

He nodded. "I suppose you have a point. It has been some time since I have left my work at work. It's rather nice, don't you think?"

I placed my hand on his neck and ran my thumb across his jawline. "Yes, it is." I gave him a little kiss and then broke the news to him. "I have had a wonderful time with you, but I have to get going. Annie and I have plans tonight. I need to get home and get showered and changed."

His hand stopped and wrapped around my leg. "You would rather go hang out with Annie than stay here with me?"

His tone was so sad. I almost felt bad telling him I had to go, but Annie would kill me if I didn't show up tonight. That didn't mean that I couldn't come back later; Annie and I always finished decently early.

"I have to go, but I can come back afterward if that's okay with you?"

He resumed running his hand up and down my leg. "I would like that." He leaned down, grabbed my chin, and kissed me. There was so much passion in his kiss it was breathtaking.

I gave him back a light kiss and then got up and walked toward his bedroom. I found my clothes and walked into the bathroom. I looked in the mirror; I didn't want to go. I hugged myself for a second, and then I changed into my clothes.

Looking at myself in daylight, I could kill Annie! This dress didn't cover a damn thing! I pulled at the hem, and the girls came out more. I could not go out like, this but I didn't have a choice.

I walked back into the bedroom and found James sitting on the bed and holding my panties up.

"Missing something?"

I laughed and walked toward him. He tossed the panties at me as he walked into the closet. He came back out while I was bending over to put on my panties.

"As much as I love this dress on you, I don't think you are going out like that." He motioned for me to raise my arms, and I did as asked. He pulled another T-shirt over my head and then pulled my dress's hem down as much as it would go.

"That's better!"

I laughed. "Care to explain why you just did that?"

He laughed too. "I'm just making sure you look decent to be out during the day. As much as I love that dress, I would prefer you wore it only when I'm around."

As much as I wanted to argue, he had a point. I had said the same thing to myself not more than two minutes ago in the bathroom. I shook my head and hugged him. I got up on my tiptoes, kissed him, and said, "And they say chivalry is dead." I walked out of the bedroom, slipped on my heels, and grabbed my purse.

He followed me out and said, "My driver is downstairs. He is ready to take you home." He pulled my phone out of my hand and typed something in it. "I saved his number as one of your favorites in case you ever need him."

Chapter 8

I walked through the front door of the apartment and found Annie in the kitchen. I set my purse and cell on the counter before walking over to the fridge and grabbing a bottle of water.

Annie gave me a once-over. "Um, care to explain?"

I laughed. "I would love to, but I have to shower, or else we are going to be late."

I walked to my bedroom and looked for something to wear. I couldn't believe it had been three years since that dreadful night. I was stuck in such a beautiful bubble with James that I hadn't even realized today was the day. Three years ago, our friend Joe Hunt was killed in a car accident. Every year since, we honored him on his birthday by doing all of the things he loved to do.

I chose a low-key outfit. I jumped in the shower, stood under the hot water, and let it take me over.

***

"Annie! Come on; we can meet up with the guys later! I just want to go get a copy of this book signed! I know Joe wants us to drive him, but he can drive himself, and I'll drive him back."

Annie protested for a bit, but finally gave in and said, "Okay, but we are leaving as soon as we get the books signed!"

We caught a cab out to the book signing; that way, we could drive Joe back home. We lucked out and were near the front of the line to get our books signed. We walked out of the bookstore and hailed a cab. We gave the driver the address.

As we pulled up to the restaurant and paid the driver, we saw Joe pull up at the stoplight. The cab dropped us off on the opposite side of the street, so we had to cross it. Joe's light turned green, and he began turning the corner. Just then, another vehicle came speeding around the corner and hit Joe head-on.

Annie and I both screamed and ran to the collision site. I dialed 911 while we tried to open the driver's door. It was jammed, and I could tell Joe was trapped. He was unconscious and bleeding. I was able to open the back door and jump in to try and get a pulse.

"Joe! Joe! Can you hear me?! Joe, please answer me!!"

I felt around for his pulse, but I couldn't find one. The paramedics arrived, and I told them that I couldn't get a read on his pulse. I advised them that I had not moved him, but I could see his leg had an open fracture, and he was pinned.

***

"Christy! Are you almost done in there?" Annie opened the door and snapped me out of my memory.

"Yeah, I'm just finishing up."

She said okay and then closed the door.

I finished up in the shower, but the memory lingered in my mind. The last three years had been hard. There was not a day that went by that I didn't blame myself for what happened to Joe. I know it's irrational because I wasn't the one who hit him, but if I had not wanted to go to that damn book signing, maybe things would have been different. Maybe Joe would still be with us.

The first year was probably the most difficult for me. I spiraled badly, and if it weren't for Mike and Annie, I might not have made it out alive. They were my greatest supporters, and I am extremely grateful for them every day.

I finished getting dressed and went back to the bathroom to blow-dry my hair a bit, and then I put it up in a messy ponytail. I hadn't realized, but I had been crying while reliving the memory. I grabbed a clean hand towel and washed my face.

Annie walked in, saw my eyes, and pulled me into a hug. "Hey, babe, it's going to be okay. I know today is a hard day, but it's going to be all right."

I hugged her tight, and she quieted me like a baby. I stopped crying and gave her a tight squeeze. "I know; it just gets me every time I think about him."

I looked at Annie; she had chosen a similar outfit, and I couldn't help but laugh. The very first night we met Joe, he ran into us in the residence's lobby, and we were two little sophomores who didn't know anything outside of the library. It was Friday night; we had just finished a study session and were sitting in the lobby, trying to figure out what movie to go watch.

Joe walked in and was on his cell phone, pacing and talking about a party. When he finally got off the phone, he was standing right in front of us. "Hey, why the long faces? You two look like you could use some fun! Hi, I'm Joe!" He extended a hand out to me, and I shook it. Then he turned to Annie and did the same.

I responded to his question, "We are looking for a good movie to watch."

He let out a laugh. "Are you serious? It's Friday night! You all should be out partying."

Annie and I had never been much for the party scene, so Annie answered for us, "We don't party much."

Joe looked at us with wild eyes. "WHAT?! What do you mean, you don't party? You all are in college! You are supposed to be out partying! Come on; you are both coming with me!"

Annie and I looked at each other, and we both shook our heads. But I was the one who answered this time, "We can't go with you; we aren't dressed for a party." We were wearing T-shirts, jeans, and Converses.

Joe looked us both over and said, "So what? You both look hot! It wouldn't matter if you came out wearing pajamas! Come on!" He grabbed us by the hand and pulled us out of the lobby.

That night, we ended up at some frat party at which we had a great time playing drinking games. Halfway through the night, I had to break the seal, so I wandered off to find the bathroom. I ended up getting lost and walked into some bedroom. I realized I made a mistake, and I turned around to walk out, but some guy stopped me by blocking the doorway. He was handsome, but I felt the hairs on the back of my neck stand up.

So I said, "Excuse me. I was looking for the bathroom," and I tried to make my way around him. He blocked me again.

"What's the rush? There is a line. Why don't you hang out with me while it dwindles down a bit?"

I shook my head, but I was a bit buzzed, and it made me a tad dizzy. The guy walked farther into the room. I didn't want to be near him, so I walked backwards to put more distance between us. Unfortunately, I backed right up against the bed, and the guy pushed me down onto it. I scrambled to get up, but the guy was already on top of me, trying to pin me down. He was built, so he was way stronger than I was. He grabbed both my hands with one of his, and he started pushing my shirt up.

I started yelling, and he tried to kiss me so he could cover my mouth. I bit him and yelled when he pulled away.

"You little bi—"

The door flew open, and Joe ran in. He pushed the guy off me and punched him a couple of times. Annie, Mike, Luke, and John were right behind him. Annie grabbed me off the bed and looked me over while the guys beat the stranger who attacked me. Annie called the cops and told them to stop.

The guys looked as if they could kill that dude, but I didn't want their lives to be ruined. "STOP IT!!! All of you! The police are on their way, and he will pay for what he's done. I don't need you all to be arrested too."

They stopped, but I knew they didn't want to. The guy lay on the floor until the cops finally came in. They broke up the party and took our statements. I told them I wanted to press charges for sexual assault. They ended up taking me to the hospital for a rape kit. I explained to them that he didn't get that far, but they said it was protocol. It was a horrible experience, but they all went with me.

That night was one of the worst nights of my life, but also one of the best. I made a very dear friend, and I wouldn't change that for the world. Tonight, however, was about Joe.

My eyes were swollen from crying; Annie helped me reduce it, and then we grabbed our purses and headed out the door. We took a cab to the restaurant to which Joe had wanted to eat that night. It was a tradition for us. Every year on his birthday, we went to Callie's. It was a bar and grill that felt more like a bar, and it had amazing food. We hung out there for a few hours before we went to the park and set up a projector; then we lay on the grass and watched a movie. This year, however, we would be watching a movie at the cemetery so we could share it with Joe.

It was an extremely simple evening, but it was what Joe always wanted to do. He was a big party animal, but on special occasions, he was more of a low-key kind of guy. I think that's one of the things that made him such a great guy.

We pulled up to Callie's and stood outside for a few minutes before we got the courage to go inside. Callie, the owner, set aside a section for us every year so we could celebrate the beautiful life that was taken too soon by a drunk driver that sneaked out of her bar before the cab could pick him up. I think she felt responsible in some way for the loss of Joe. The party was small, but it included those who mattered most—Mike, Annie, Luke, John and I were the only ones in attendance. We had dinner, but not one of us drank alcohol. It was a tribute.

At around 7:30 p.m., we left Callie's and headed to the cemetery. Annie and I picked up some flowers from around the corner, while the guys went to set up the projector. By the time we got there, the guys had everything set up and the blankets laid out. Annie and I set the flowers up by Joe's tombstone and wished him a happy birthday. I lay against the tombstone, and Annie lay on my lap. We said a prayer and sang happy birthday. Once everyone was settled in, we started the movie. It was some comedy. Joe was big on laughter; if people weren't laughing, he found a way to make them.

The caretaker knew that for the last three years we had done the same thing. It was against the rules to do this type of thing, but I think he felt sorry for us. He made himself scarce for the two hours or so and then showed up with a trash bag so we could trash the evidence of food we'd sneaked in.

We all said our good-nights and headed our separate ways. Annie and I hailed a cab home. The car ride was silent, but she laid her head on my shoulder; I could hear her sniffling. I rested my head atop hers and just let the tears fall. By the time we got home, both of us were a wreck. We got inside and sat on the couch hugging each other until the tears stopped.

Annie excused herself to go to bed. I went to the bathroom to freshen up because I told James I would come back over tonight. I had a feeling, if I didn't show up, he would come look for me.

The good thing was that I always asked for the week off that led up to or followed the anniversary. Annie did the same thing. As much as we loved being roommates, we both needed some time off to deal with the loss of Joe. We both witnessed it firsthand, and we never knew how to deal with it. Last year, she went to the Bahamas for a week, and I went to Ireland. We never told each other where we planned to go. We just caught up after the trip. It was like a cleansing, if you will. Christopher and Blake were aware of the situation and very understanding.

I grabbed my suitcase; it had been packed for a week now. I hadn't made up my mind if or where I was going, but I had booked a ticket to Italy just in case. If I decided to go, I would depart Sunday at midnight. I left a note on the kitchen island for Annie, explaining that I was off for the week and that I would catch up with her when I got back.

***

I stepped onto the curb and looked up at the apartment building in front of me. *I really shouldn't be here tonight. I'm too exposed, and it could turn out very badly.* I thought about turning back to the cab, but he was just pulling away. *Too late now.*

I walked up to the security desk, and the security guard greeted me by name; he told me to go right ahead. I was going to question him about it, but what was the point?

I am sure James told him he was expecting me at some point tonight.

I rode the elevator up to the top floor, and there he was when the doors opened. He arched an eyebrow when he saw my suitcase, but grabbed it from me anyway, and pulled me out of the elevator and into a giant hug. He set me down and grabbed both sides of my face. "Are you all right? What's wrong? Have you been crying?"

I knew this was going to happen, but if I hadn't come, James would have searched for me, and then he would have been dealing with both Annie and me. I leaned into his hand and nodded my head.

He picked me up and walked me over to the couch. "Are you all right?"

I nodded my head. "I am fine. I didn't want you to see me like this, so I wasn't going to come back tonight. But then I realized that if I didn't come back, you might go look for me, and I really didn't want that either."

He gave me a squeeze and said, "Damn right, I would have looked for you! Tell me why you have been crying! Did someone hurt you?!"

I could see he was working himself up, so I shook my head and regained as much composure as I could. "No one hurt me. I am all right. It's a long story, and one I am not currently willing to share. You arched an eyebrow when you saw my suitcase. Just so you know, I am not planning on moving in here with you or anything. I am actually going on vacation. I leave Sunday at midnight. I wasn't sure I was going to make it home before my flight, so I just brought my stuff with me."

He studied me for a bit before he responded, "You are going on vacation? What about the campaign?"

I smiled gently at him. "Charlie and the rest of the team will have everything under control. I have no concerns about them getting the job done. Plus, I will only be gone a week."

He thought about it for a little bit. "When were you going to tell me that you were going on vacation? Or were you going to tell me at all?"

I shook my head. "Up until yesterday, I didn't have a reason to tell you I was going anywhere. You were my client, and there was no reason for you to know." I could tell he didn't like that answer, but he nodded.

It wasn't until then that I noticed he was wearing the same shirt I had been wearing all morning. He had on different pajama bottoms, but it was definitely the same shirt. It made me feel warm inside, and I started giggling.

He arched an eyebrow again. "What on earth are you laughing at?"

It took me a bit to catch my breath, and then I pointed to the shirt. "Is that the shirt I was wearing this morning?"

I could have sworn he blushed! "Yes, it's one of my favorite shirts."

Now, I was the one arching an eyebrow. "Has it always been one of your favorite shirts, or is it just your favorite because I wore it all morning?"

He gave me a devilish grin and then launched himself on top of me. It was playful, but I couldn't help associating it with that night many years ago, and I freaked! I started pushing at him and hyperventilating.

He immediately got up and sat me up, but I was already in a full-blown panic attack. I couldn't catch my breath, and he was freaking out! I was trying to slow my breathing, but it was hard. I put my head between my legs to slow the attack, but it wasn't working. I tried to get up and get to my purse, but I just fell back on the couch. He was trying to get me to stay put, so I vigorously pointed at my purse.

He ran, grabbed it, and poured everything on the coffee table. My inhaler was the last thing to fall out. He grabbed it and shoved it in my hand. I took a good first puff and started slowing my breaths. It helped, and I started to feel a bit better. Once my breathing was more controlled, I took the second puff, and it settled me down all the way.

There was no way I was going to get away with not explaining this to James. Aside from being the anniversary of Joe's death, it was also the anniversary of my assault. Days apart, but nonetheless the same week. *Damn it, Christy! You couldn't hold it together until you got to Italy?! Now you have to explain everything to him!*

James brought me a glass of water and sat on the coffee table across from me. "Are you all right? Do you need anything?"

I scared him half to death I could see it in his eyes. They were filled with concern. I was mortified. How could I not explain now? I didn't want him thinking it was because of him. I set the glass and my inhaler down on the table and grabbed his hands in mine.

"I am all right. I'm sorry you had to see that."

He shook his head. "Why on earth are you apologizing? I should be the one to apologize!"

I squeezed his hands. "Earlier, you asked me why I was crying. I really didn't want to talk about it, and I still don't. It's not easy for me, but I feel I owe you an explanation. This time of year is very difficult for me. I moved thousands of miles away from home with no one but my childhood best friend. I was fortunate to meet Annie my freshman year of college, and since then, she has become my sister. Life was hard, but Annie and my friend from home made it better. I devoted my time to studying and being in the library. Our entire freshman year, we spent eighty-five percent of our time in the library. When sophomore year came around, it was about the same until spring semester during this week of that year.

"It was a Friday night, and Annie and I had just finished a study session. We were in the residence's lobby, trying to figure out what movie to go watch. Then, a boy walked in, and he paced while talking on his cell. After his conversation, he came over to talk to us. He introduced himself; his name was Joe. He asked what we were doing, and we told him looking for a movie. He said that we needed to experience life and that we need to do some partying during our college years.

"He took us to a frat party. He never let us out of his sight. He brought us closed-bottle drinks that we had to open ourselves so that we knew they weren't tampered with and everything. We were playing drinking games, and I had to go to the bathroom. He told me exactly where it was and told me not to deviate. I had a light buzz, but nothing too bad.

"I followed his instructions, but I got turned around and ended up walking into a bedroom instead of a bathroom. When I turned around, there was some guy blocking the doorway. I excused myself and tried to get out, but he blocked my exit and started walking toward me. I felt the hairs on the back of my neck rise, so I started to walk backward away from him. Unfortunately, I ended up walking straight to the bed, and he pushed me and got on top of me. He was much stronger than I was, and he pinned me down. I began screaming, and he tried to kiss me to shut me up. I bit him and started screaming again.

"He had already pulled my shirt up and grabbed my breast, but as I was screaming, Joe busted in and pulled the guy off me. Annie and the rest of my friends walked in after him, and they beat him up until I yelled at them to stop so they wouldn't go to jail. Annie called the cops, and, well, it was a bit of a mess after that. I had to be taken to the ER to have a rape kit done, even though I told them he didn't get that far. They said it was protocol. It was a horrible night for me. One that I have tried to cope with for a long time. It's still pretty hard for me."

James looked horrified. He was frozen in place and looked as if he were very far away. I squeezed his hand, and he began apologizing. "I am so sorry, Christy! I didn't mean to hurt you like that. I am so, so sorry!"

I shook my head and grabbed both his hands again. "James, you have nothing to apologize for. You didn't know, and you didn't do anything wrong."

I hugged him, and he just sat there. It was horrible! He didn't want to react around me or didn't know how to.

"James, I need you to say something or hug me."

He snapped out of it and hugged me. He gave me a squeeze and then pushed me back a little to look at me. He gave me a once-over to see if I was really fine.

"Since that night, Joe and the rest of our group have become really good friends. Joe checked in on me almost every hour on the hour for the next month! He blamed himself for what happened, and it took a long time for me to convince him otherwise. He made sure I never felt alone or vulnerable. He was the one that got me into the gym and lifting weights. He knew that I blamed myself for being an easy target, so he tried to help with that.

"Today is his birthday." I let that sink in for a little bit. I thought it might be too much for James to handle, so I stopped.

He stared at me and then said, "Why are you not out celebrating with him?"

I felt a knot in my throat. It was almost as if James knew there was more to come. My eyes got watery, but I fought through the tears.

"Three years ago today, I was supposed to be Joe's designated driver. However, my favorite author was in town, and I wanted to go get my book signed. I convinced Annie to come with me. I told her it would be quick, and I could still be the DD. Joe said it was fine. He told us to just meet him at the restaurant, and then he would hand over the keys.

"Annie and I got to the book signing really early, so we were in and out. We caught a cab to the restaurant and got there at the exact time Joe did. He pulled up at the stoplight when we got dropped off across the street. We were at the crosswalk when Joe's light turned green. He was mid-turn when some idiot came speeding down the street and crashed into him head-on. I called 911 and then ran to the car and tried to pry the door open. I couldn't. I was able to open the back door, so I jumped in and tried to wake up Joe. There was a lot of blood, and I couldn't find a pulse. He had an open leg fracture, and he was pinned in.

"When the paramedics and the firefighters got there, they pulled him out and transported him to the hospital. He didn't make it. I rode with him in the ambulance, but he was gone before we got to the hospital."

I couldn't help it anymore. I started crying like a baby again. Telling Joe's last story was too much for me. It had been three years, and I still couldn't cope.

James sat next to me on the couch and picked me up. He set me on his lap and pulled me close. He wrapped his arms around me and rocked me back and forth. I truly felt like a baby, but it was soothing. He made me feel safe. He rocked me in silence until I stopped sobbing and was only sniffling.

"I am really sorry for your loss, honey. I am really sorry about all of it. You have been through a lot, and I'm sorry you had to relive it just now."

He set me down on the couch and went into the kitchen. When he came back he was carrying a cup of tea. "Here, drink this; it should help you relax."

We sat there in silence until I finished my tea. When I was done, he took the cup from my hand and set it on the coffee table. He stood up and held out a hand for me. I took it, and he pulled me up. We walked to the bedroom, and he helped me undress. Once I was down to my undergarments, he pulled his T-shirt off and put it on me again. Then we got into bed. He pulled me close and just held me while I sniffled myself to sleep.

Chapter 9

I felt the sun on my face and the warmth of James behind me. I was so toasty that I didn't want to move. I opened my eyes and peeked over my shoulder to find James watching me.

"Good morning, Sleeping Beauty!" He kissed my cheek.

I blushed and snuggled closer to him. "Good morning, Beast!"

He laughed! "That's the wrong fairy tale, my dear."

I turned over to look at him and ran my thumb along his jawline. "I know."

He lowered his head and planted a soft kiss on my lips. "How are you feeling this morning?"

I played with the stubble on his cheek, and I could feel him watching me. The truth was, I still felt pretty rotten. It had been a long night. Although I didn't have nightmares—or at least I didn't remember them if I did—I felt as if I hadn't slept at all. "I'm okay."

He arched an eyebrow. "Are you? You didn't sleep very well last night."

So I did have nightmares, damn it! I remember some of the ones I used to have, and they were awful! I used to talk in my sleep, and Joe would climb up on the bed and hold me until I cried myself to sleep.

I had to know if James heard anything. "What do you mean?"

I saw a pained expression cross his face for a second until he composed himself. He tucked a strand of hair behind my ear. "Honey, do you think it will do you any good to know if you don't remember?"

Now, I know I talked in my sleep. Nothing would cause him to have that expression on his face or want to dance around the question.

"Please tell me. It might not do me any good to know, but I use these things to help me cope."

He had his hand on my hip and gave me a gentle squeeze. "At first, it was mild noises. You were whimpering, and then you started kicking and saying no a lot. I wanted to hold you, but I didn't think it would be a good idea. Instead, I held your hand and kissed your cheek. I think it helped because you settled down and stopped kicking. You were still whimpering, but no longer yelling or kicking. I took advantage of hugging you at that time, and you ended up quieting and falling asleep."

Oh man, I really didn't want him to see that, but at least it was a mild episode. Which makes me think the worst ones are yet to come. I don't want to leave, but it's important that I get this under control so that I am able to keep seeing James without scaring the life out of him.

I turned over to face the ceiling, closed my eyes, and blew out a breath. *I know that James and I aren't really anything major, much less exclusive, so he doesn't get a say in what I do, but I feel strange going on a trip without him.*

James let me be for what I imagine was as long as he could stand it, but then he rolled on top of me and started kissing my cheek. It was playful, and I stayed relaxed, with my eyes closed, as long as I could, but then his hands started roaming around. It was strange that I didn't feel any anxiety with him, even after last night. His touch was gentle and warm. He trailed his hand up and down my leg while peppering my neck with kisses. It felt amazing, and I couldn't resist him any longer. I tilted my head away from him to give him a better vantage point, and he accepted the invitation.

An hour later, I excused myself to take a shower. I needed some alone time to think. My flight left at midnight, and he still hadn't said anything about my leaving. *Does he even care that I am leaving?* I stopped that line of thinking before I got too far. *James and I are not exclusive, and if he doesn't care that I will be gone for a week, then it's okay.*

On a sidenote, his shower was amazing! I didn't have time to appreciate it before, but wow! It had power jets, and the thermostat was wonderful! I really enjoyed being under the waterfall.

I took what I thought was an appropriate amount of time in the shower and then got dressed and made my way to the kitchen. My stomach was growling, and it was embarrassing how loud it actually was. I could smell the coffee and something else I couldn't quite make out.

I found James in front of the stove. I walked up to him and hugged him from behind. He turned halfway and put an arm around me. It allowed me to peek, and I found it was waffles! *I love waffles!!! How on earth did he know?!*

I kissed his chest and untangled myself from his arm so I could get some coffee in me before my stomach decided to make another noise. Once I had a few sips of coffee, I made my way to the fridge to find some fruit. I took out some apples and strawberries so I could wash and cut them up. I finished with the fruit just in time.

James placed the plates on the island, and I added the fruit. He looked up at me and started laughing. I am almost positive I had a goofy grin on my face. I couldn't help it though. I love waffles! I shoved him a little, and he rewarded me with a kiss.

"I take it you love waffles too?"

I gave him a huge smile and a kiss on the cheek! "Yes!" I grabbed my plate and went to go sit on the other side of the island.

He watched me curiously. "I thought you didn't sit down when you ate breakfast?"

I shrugged. "This is different. Waffles are life!"

He couldn't help but laugh hysterically. Once he recovered from his bout of laughter, he said, "Note taken!"

I meant what I said about waffles being life. I sat there and cut them up into small pieces and actually chewed each individual piece about twenty-five times before I swallowed. I loved waffles. My mom used to make me waffles every Sunday when I was a kid. The only times she didn't was when she had to work or when I was grounded. The latter was very rare.

James finished eating about as soon as he began and then turned to watch me intently. "I've seen you eat a few times, and from those few times, I have never seen you eat this slowly. This waffle thing must be pretty serious for you to chew that many times."

There was humor in his tone, and I thought about countering with something witty, but what could I rebut with? I smiled and nodded instead. I could tell he wanted to say more, but instead just kept me company while I finished eating.

After breakfast, I washed the dishes, and he dried and put them away. I was surprised at how domestic this man was. For all the money he made, on weekends, he sure didn't act as if he had any. We went over to the living room. He sat on the same corner of the couch as yesterday, and I laid my head on his lap. We watched TV for a little while before I dozed off.

I opened my eyes to find I was alone in the living room. The TV was on, but the volume was very low. I could hear James talking to someone, but I couldn't make out what he was saying. I thought about getting up and going to go find him, but then remembered that it was none of my business.

I instead sat up and went to grab my tablet from my suitcase. I powered it on and began arranging my flight check-in and car service. I had just finished finalizing the arrangements when James walked into the living room.

He was surprised to find me awake. "You're up."

I smiled and nodded.

"Why didn't you come find me when you woke up?" he asked.

I powered off the tablet and set it aside. "Because I heard you talking, and I didn't want to interrupt. Plus, I needed to get some stuff done, so it worked out."

He walked over to me and sat beside me. "Everything okay?"

I nodded and leaned into him. It was crazy how easy it was to be around him now. Before, I couldn't even breathe properly if I knew he was in the same building, for fear of running into him.

He hugged me. "So where are you off to on your vacation?"

I thought about his question before I answered. I wanted to tell him where I was going, but I didn't think it was a good idea. I might be a bit paranoid, but if he found out where I was going, he might actually show up there, but the purpose of this trip was to get away from my everyday life. It was a chance for me to be anyone I wanted to be. A part of me wanted to tell him, but the other part told me to keep it a secret.

I decided to be playful about it. "I'd tell ya, but then I'd have to kill ya."

He narrowed his eyes and stared at me for a bit.

Rather than let him answer, I decided to explain. "For the last three years, Annie and I have gone on vacations anonymously. We tell each other and our families that we are going out of town, and we will be unreachable for about a week. Neither of us discloses the location we are off to until we return. We use this time to unwind, but also to review our lives and assess how they are going.

"I personally have been through a lot, and I enjoy taking these vacations because they help nurture a part of my soul. So please understand that I would love to tell you where I'm going, but the fact is, it's best if you don't know."

I could see his mind working, and I knew he wanted to argue about it, but he simply nodded and pulled me closer.

We lay on the couch, being lazy, all day, and when 3:30 p.m. rolled around, I started kissing his chest. They were light kisses, but long enough to be sensual. I made my way up to his neck and then back down to his navel. I could tell he was enjoying it because the crotch area of his pants tented.

As I continued kissing him, I let my hand navigate toward his pajama bottoms. I untied the string and put my hand in his pants. As I suspected, he was not wearing any underwear. I ran my hand up and down his dick. I couldn't fathom how large he was. I pulled it out and leaned down to take it into my mouth. James lay there with his head tilted back, and I knew he was enjoying himself. I caressed his penis with my tongue. I moved my head up and down slowly and swiped with my tongue while my hand juggled his balls. When I felt him start tensing, I knew it was time to go deeper.

I repositioned myself and took him farther into my mouth until his cock touched the back of my throat. I sucked him while increasing my speed in small increments until I felt the warm gooeyness slide down my throat. I slowed until he was spent. I licked him clean and topped it off with a kiss to the tip.

Because, after my shower, I hadn't bothered to put on anything other than one of James's T-shirts, I straddled him and pulled the T-shirt off in a striptease kind of way. His head was still tilted back, and I took advantage of kissing his neck and jawline. I could tell he was still recovering, but he didn't waste time in grabbing my waist.

He ran his fingers up and down my sides for a little bit before he started to play with my breasts. He rolled my nipples between his thumbs and index fingers until they were taut. There was something about that that made me so hot. He had barely touched me, and I was already wet. It was crazy how he had that effect on me. He replaced one of his hands with his mouth while his hand wandered down between my legs.

It was irritating how slowly his hand was traveling, and I think he realized I was anxious for him to get there already. He redirected his hand and ran it up and down my leg, and then up and down my back. It was extremely hot and frustrating at the same time.

I was kissing his neck right below his ear, and as he continued to tease me, I nipped his earlobe. Luckily, he took that as a hint, and finally his hand made its way in between us. He stroked gently on the sides of my labia and then began making his way into my inner folds. His fingers slipped around easily.

"Honey, I love that you get so wet and ready for me." He inserted a finger and moved in and out until he felt he could add another one. It expanded my opening and felt incredible. He switched boobs and moved his hand to play with my clitoris. It was sensational, and I felt as if I was ready to climax. He played a little longer before he shoved his finger inside me, and that pushed me over the edge.

As I was coming down from my climax, he shoved his dick inside me, and it reignited my passion. He wrapped an arm around my waist and leaned me away from him to allow for a better fit. By doing so, he was able to push all the way inside. I was so full, and it felt amazing. It was a bit painful, but the pleasurable kind of pain. We estab-lished a rhythm and moved at that pace until he was ready again. I could feel him twitch inside me, and it made me start twitching. I was starting to climax again.

He reached between us and said, "Stay with me," as he started rubbing my clit between his thumb and his index finger.

It was too much for me. I let out a shout and came in a rush. He pulled me toward him as we both rode out our orgasms.

I lay against his chest while he was still inside me. It was incredible and just what I needed. I knew I would have to get up soon to start getting ready, but I didn't want to move. He filled me just perfectly, and the thought of not being able to have this for a whole week was almost devastating.

James must have been thinking the same thing because he said, "I wish you didn't have to go."

I nodded my head because I couldn't speak without being emotional.

He kissed my cheek and held me. We sat there like that for about an hour until he told me it was best if I went and got ready.

We had a light dinner before he escorted me to the airport. He wanted to come inside with me, but I told him it was better he didn't. When my suitcase was out of the trunk and on the curb next to me, I got on my tiptoes and gave him a gentle kiss.

Before I could get away, he pulled me into his embrace and deepened the kiss. It wasn't until we heard a car horn blaring that we broke for air. We both laughed, and I gave him one last peck and walked away. When I was inside, I stepped out of his line of sight and watched him leave. I wanted to make sure he left before I boarded. I knew I was being paranoid, but I needed to be alone this week.

Once I saw him drive away, I went to my gate. It was still early, and my flight was on time. I decided to go to the gift shop to see what kind of unnecessary knickknacks I could find. I never bought the damn things, but they were fun to play with and pass the time.

As I was about to enter the gift shop, I got a text message. Come to find out, it was James.

Really wish you didn't have to go. Have fun and be safe! See you soon. Xoxo.

He was so sweet! I sent him a quick reply and headed into the store. I looked around, but I wasn't able to find anything interesting. When I was certain I had roamed the entire store, I decided to go back to my gate. There were more people filing in as the time got closer to departure.

I decided it would be a good idea to call Mike. He was not a fan of the yearly getaways. He believed they were unhealthy for both Annie and me. I supposed he could have a point, but it was the way we knew how to cope.

"Hello," he said.

It was weird; I didn't know what to say.

"Hello? Christy?" he said again.

I exhaled. "Hey, Mikey! I just wanted to call and let you know it's about that time again. I'm heading off, and I should be back in a week or so. If you need me, please email me!"

I could hear him blow out a breath he must have been holding. "Christy, again? I thought we talked about this. You all have to learn to cope differently! You can't keep running away from your problems just because you have the means to. It's not healthy. I know it's too late for this year, but when you all get back, I am taking you all to a shrink to help you learn how to cope and forgive. Fly safe, and please be careful!"

I mindlessly responded to him and hung up before he found out where I was off to. He had a point, but I don't think I was ready to deal with all that guilt. Not when pretending and ignoring was easier. The plane was ready for departure, and it was going to be a long flight. I grabbed my carry-on and pillow and boarded the plane.

* * *

The captain announced over the intercom, "Good morning, everyone! We are cleared to land in Venice. Please return to your seats and buckle up."

I straightened up and fastened my seat belt. The landing was smooth, and as I got up, I realized I had slept wrong because I was sore in all the wrong places. I exited the plane and made my way to the cabstand. I needed to get to the hotel so I could take a shower, get a massage, and eat some breakfast. I hailed a taxi and gave him the name of my hotel—the Hilton Molino Stucky Venice. I had done extensive research on where to stay, and this place offered the most amenities and had the best reviews. I made sure that, every time I went on vacation, I chose hotels that were the safest since I would be by myself for at least a week. When the taxi driver dropped me off, I thanked and paid him. I checked in, and the bellhop helped me with my bag.

The room was incredible! It was done in warm colors that made you feel as if you were home, and the view was of the canal. The bed was extremely soft and comfy. I unpacked and made my way to the bathroom. It was spacious, and the tub and shower were separate. I contemplated taking a bath, but since I wanted to go to the spa, I opted for a shower.

The water felt amazing on my skin! I stood under the showerhead for what felt like a really long time, but it turned out to be about five minutes. After my shower, I dressed in a jogging outfit and headed down for breakfast. I sat at a small table and waited for a waiter. When she came up to my table, I greeted her, *"Buongiorno! Come stai questa mattina?"*

She appeared surprised that I spoke Italian. I had been practicing for a while now, but I was very limited. She replied, "*Facendo bene.* Come stai? *Posso portarti qualcosa da bere?*"

It took me a second to remember what she was asking me, but then I responded, "*Caffè e acqua.*"

She smiled at me. "*Va bene. Tornerò.*" She walked away.

I exhaled and pulled out my phone. I normally didn't pay for the international service, but I felt it appropriate this time around. I didn't plan on calling anyone, but I wanted to see what was going on back home. I turned on my cell phone and set it down so it could boot up.

The waitress came back and set down my coffee and water. I asked her for some scrambled eggs and toast, and she walked away.

My phone beeped. I picked it up and found a few text messages. There were some from Annie, Luke, Mike, Christopher, Blake, and, last but not least, James. I went down the line, opening messages. Annie's were simple, just wishing me a safe trip and telling me to have fun. I responded with similar wishes and moved on to Luke's message. Luke's was more complicated; he asked how and where I was and why I hadn't responded to his calls or messages.

I responded with a quick, *It's that time of year. I'll be back in a week, and we can talk then.*

Christopher, Blake, and I were in a group message. They were making sure I landed safely and telling me to let them know if I needed anything. Mike's message was similar to Annie's. I typed a quick response and then went on to the message I really wanted to read.

I opened James's text to find a picture of his empty bed with rumpled covers. The message read: *Missing you! Hope you have a safe, fun, and short trip! See you soon!*

I was laughing when the waitress brought my breakfast. I smiled at her and then typed a message back to him: *I'm missing you too! See you soon, but for now, check the nightstand drawer.* I had left him five new pocket squares, each with a splash of my perfume, for him to wear during this week. I know that's probably a little more on the relationship side of things, but I didn't care; it felt right.

I hadn't realized how much I missed him until right then. I pushed my breakfast around and sipped on my coffee. I wasn't hungry. I left money on the table for the breakfast and made my way down to the spa. Maybe some relaxation would help me take my mind off James.

The spa was incredible, but the traveling was beginning to take its toll. I had gone out for some sightseeing, but I was so tired. I went upstairs, ordered room service, and drew a bath. I dimmed the lights, lit scented candles, and was selecting a playlist for relaxation when my phone started ringing.

It was James; he was not going to make this easy. I answered, "Hello?" I could hear him talking to someone. I waited for a second to make sure it wasn't a butt-dial. It wasn't.

"Christy? Are you there?"

I laid my head back and closed my eyes. "Mm-hmm."

The line went silent, and then I heard him inhale deeply. "What are you doing, darling?" His voice was so velvety it made me all warm and fuzzy.

"Wouldn't you like to know?"

I could imagine his brow furrowing. "Yes, actually I *would* like to know."

I giggled a bit and then decided it would be best just to tell him what I was doing. "I am taking a bath. The flight was long, and I think I slept wrong because I was completely sore in all the wrong places. I went and got a massage, and it helped. So I figured I would finish out the day with a bath before bed."

He was quiet, and I couldn't help but imagine him getting hard. I really needed to stop my mind from getting down in the gutter. "I wish I was there with you. I would sit behind you, rub your shoulders, and pepper you with kisses."

I could imagine him doing just that. This week was going to be really hard if I kept answering his messages and taking his calls. "James, you are making this really hard for me." I felt horrible saying it, but I had to.

He laughed. "Good, that's the point. I have no idea where you are, but I'm guessing that you are somewhere in Europe. I am struggling being away from you, and it doesn't seem to be a struggle for you at all."

I exhaled. "I have to let you go, James. Room service just arrived. Have a good one!"

I hung up before he had the chance to say something charming. I also turned off my phone for good measure. This trip's sole purpose was to get away from everything to try to put the past in perspective.

I am going to pay for hanging up on him and turning off my phone, but I don't care. I got out of the bath and rinsed off in the shower. When I put the robe on and walked into the bedroom, I found that room service had indeed been there. I ate and then fell asleep.

I felt as if I had slept for days. When I woke up, the sun was shining bright. I felt relaxed already. I got out of bed and went to get ready. It was time to see what Italy had to offer! I had packed light summer clothing and a few workout outfits. I wasn't sure if I was going to do some hiking through the country or not. I picked a tank top, some shorts, and my Converses. I grabbed my crossbody purse and made my way downstairs. I wanted to capture everything Italian!

The first few days I stayed local and checked out all of the architecture. It amazed me how varied it was here, and the food was incredible! I think, if it were not for all of the walking, I might actually gain weight. The art museums held so much history, and the tour guides were very knowledgeable.

I had flown into Venice, but my flight home was from Rome. So I spent the next couple of days traveling through the countryside. I spent a few hours in Bologna; they had exquisite cuisine. Then I travelled down to Siena. Although I missed the famous Palio horse race, the city itself did not disappoint. The architecture was incredible. The city is seated on three hills, and in the center is the Piazza del Campo.

The day had been pretty long, and the driving took a lot out of me. I decided to spend two days in Siena. I wanted to climb up the Torre del Mangia. I was in no shape to climb some 500 steps, but what the heck. I didn't see myself coming back here anytime soon. It took me quite a while to get up those steps, but the view was extraordinary! I could see for miles and miles! It was definitely worth climbing my ass up there. The climb took a lot out of me.

I was able to sleep in the next day. I had paid for a late checkout. Luckily, to them, that was 3:00 p.m. I got back on the road at about 2:30 p.m. The drive to Rome was not that long. Worst case, I would make it there by about 6:00 p.m. Just in time for dinner and to catch up on some sleep. I wanted to see Rome in its entirety before I had to head back to the States.

I woke up bright and early and had a light breakfast. I wanted not only to see everything, but also to eat everything. I visited the Colosseum, the Pantheon, and the Trevi Fountain, where I found some amazing gelato. I checked out the Vatican's museums, St. Peter's Basilica, and the Sistine Chapel. Everything was just beautiful! I ate at little hole-in-the-wall places that had the most amazing pasta. I thought I knew what Italian cuisine was, but I am not sure I could look at pasta the same way after this trip.

As the day wound down, I made my way over to the Fontana dei Quattro Fiumi, or the Fountain of the Four Rivers. It is said to depict the gods of the four rivers— the Nile, Ganges, Danube, and Río de la Plata. An infinite number of people gather to admire the fountain. It was truly a sight to behold. There was something about it that captivated me. I spent quite some time observing and taking photos. Once I made my way around it and was satisfied with the number of photos I had taken, I decided it was time to head back to the hotel. I had an early flight the next day, and the jet lag was going to be awful!

I had a light dinner and took a long bath before heading to bed. I woke pretty early and decided it wasn't going to do me any good to lie around. I gathered my things and checked out. I drove to the airport and dropped off the rental. Once I cleared security, I went and grabbed a coffee and a croissant and headed for my gate. It was still too early for any of my fellow stateside travelers to be here, so I picked a seat closest to the gate and camped out. I pulled out my tablet so I could start categorizing my pictures and then realized that I hadn't turned my phone back on since I spoke with James. I felt a tinge of remorse, but then reminded myself that there was nothing between us. Even though I knew deep down I was in over my head with him.

I was on the verge of turning on my phone and then thought better of it. I'd rather deal with reality once I was back in it. I messed with my tablet and organized all of my photos into categories and folders. Talk about OCD. Before I knew it, almost three hours had gone by. They called for my plane to board just as I was shutting down my tablet.

I jumped up and made my way to the front of the gate. The TSA member took my ticket and let me make my way down the ramp to board. I found my seat and settled in after storing my luggage in the overhead bins. This was going to be a long flight, but I couldn't wait to get home!

Chapter 10

The airport was buzzing by the time I deplaned. I caught a cab. It was still early, and I thought about going to James's apartment, but since I hadn't spoken to him for a few days, I didn't know what to expect. I also wasn't sure if he was there or at his estate. I ended up just giving the driver my apartment address.

When I arrived, I thought I might find Annie, but instead I found a note, on the fridge door, explaining that she wouldn't be back until Tuesday. She had decided to leave later in the week, and her trip would run into this coming week. Normally, I would love having alone time, but right now I didn't want to be alone. I felt uneasy. It was weird, but I felt as if I needed someone around.

I made my way to the bedroom and looked in the mirror. It was a horrible sight, so I decided to jump in the shower. Since Annie wouldn't be home, I dried myself and decided to stay nude. I went to check the fridge to see if there were any edible leftovers before I resorted to the takeout drawer. I sniffed around, but Annie was a stickler about not leaving food in the fridge. She threw everything out before she left. I laughed because she left a note in the takeout drawer explaining that I needed to order takeout and to make sure to put some clothes on before I answered the door.

I rummaged through the menus and settled on Chinese. The restaurant said it would be about thirty minutes. I went and grabbed a throw from my room and placed it on the couch before I sat down. I turned on the TV and was surfing the channels when I heard the doorbell. It hadn't even been ten minutes!

I got up, checked the peephole, and went weak in the knees. It was James. I stood there frozen for a bit.

And then I heard him say, "I know you're in there. Annie told me you had mentioned your flight would arrive this afternoon. Open the door."

I had the chain on the door, so I pulled it open and poked my head around the door to say hello.

He arched an eyebrow. "Are you going to let me in?"

I stared at him for what seemed like an eternity before I nodded. I closed the door, undid the chain, but didn't open the door back up. Instead, I ran back to the couch and wrapped myself in the throw.

James opened the door and looked in to find me sitting on the couch. He walked in and locked the door with the chain.

He must know that Annie isn't here.

He walked over and stood in front of the couch, looking down at me. "What are you doing? Why didn't you open the door?"

I shook my head and smiled. "You wouldn't have approved if had I opened the door while there were people walking by."

He got an evil look in his eye. He reached down and pulled at the hem of the throw hard enough to pull it out of my hand and expose my naked body. He must have missed me because he was hard before he even touched the throw. I tugged at the throw so I could cover myself back up, but James sat on the edge of it.

By the look in his eyes, he was ravenous. I was sitting with my knees tucked under my chin, and he pulled at my legs to extend and spread them. He settled between my legs, leaned forward, and laid a longing kiss on my lips. It was soft and gentle at first, but then he deepened it. His hands were everywhere; it was as if he didn't know where to touch or what to feel first.

His desire was too much for me to bear. I was wet before he even went that far. He was kissing my lips and then began trailing kisses down my neck and chest, to my navel, until he reached the junction of my legs. He blew a light, warm gust of air while using his fingers to spread my outer lips apart. He used his index finger to feel inside of me, after which he looked up immediately and said, "Someone missed me."

He was so cocky I just wanted to wipe that grin off his face, but he wasn't wrong. I missed him dearly. But before I could respond, he ducked his head between my legs and began working his wicked tongue between my folds. I'm not sure if it was because he was incredible or my body was deprived, but the orgasm was almost instantaneous!

However, I wasn't sated. I needed him *now*. I pulled James up and tugged at his sweats. I didn't have time to acknowledge the fact that he came prepared. His dick came free as soon as I pulled his pants down. I grabbed ahold of it and guided it toward my entrance. I didn't have to say anything; he pulled me up by my waist and thrust inside me in a quick rush. It was painful because it had been a while, but the feeling of pleasure after the pain was incredible. He leaned down and kissed me deeply as we moved in sync. He must have missed me too because we both came just as fast the second time.

He lay on top of me, while still inside me, until the doorbell rang again. He lifted his head to look at me with a quizzical stare.

I giggled. "It's my Chinese food! You will have to get it because I am not opening the door like this again."

He growled at me before he took bit my boob.

We ate and watched a movie before heading to bed. Italy was amazing, but there was nothing like sleeping in my own bed. I woke up feeling refreshed and warm with James next to me. I kissed him before heading to the shower.

By the time I was done, James had gotten dressed and made coffee. He kissed me and told me to have a good day at work, and we both set off separately.

I decided to walk to work and soak up the sunlight. By the time I got to work, I felt warm and was glad that I had chosen to wear a quarter-sleeve blouse with a blazer instead of my usual sleeveless blouse. I removed my blazer and placed it behind my chair.

Landon walked in. "Good morning, sunshine! Welcome back! How was the trip?"

I smiled at him. "Good morning! The trip was amazing! Italy was incredible! I highly recommend you visit it!"

His eyes lit up like a Christmas tree. "You went to Italy?! Without me?! How dare you!!!"

I laughed. "The next time I decide to go to Italy, I will take you with me! I promise!"

He nodded at me. "I'll hold you to that! However, for now, everyone is in the conference room. They would like to update you on how the campaigns are going."

I picked up my things and made my way to the conference room. I couldn't wait to see all of the ideas my team had come up with while I was away. I walked in, and everyone was hard at work. All the whiteboards were up, and drawings were hanging around the room. Everything looked incredible.

Charlie was the one who spotted me before anyone else. "Welcome back, stranger!" he shouted across the room.

Everyone looked up from their work, clapping and cheering.

It was an amazing feeling to be appreciated and missed. "Thank you, everyone! I missed you all as well! I am truly impressed with the progress you all have made! Anyone care to fill me in?"

For the next few hours, I walked around the room, met with each team, and made suggestions and revisions on each piece. Before lunchtime, I texted Landon and asked him to buy lunch for everyone. I wanted to show everyone a little bit of my appreciation.

Landon walked in with lunch, and everyone cleared the table. I helped him set up.

"Please, everyone, take a seat and grab some lunch. This is not a working lunch. I would like us to sit and chat, but not about work. We work very hard, and I think it would be nice to sit and enjoy a meal with friends."

Everyone sat and ate while talking about vacation plans. Two of the girls on the team apparently just found out that they were expecting. One was six weeks in, and the other was almost twelve. Everyone had great stories to tell. I was rather disappointed in myself. I had never taken the time to get to know anyone with whom I worked. Not truly anyway.

The rest of the day flew by. It was 6:00 p.m., and everyone had already trickled out. Annie was due to get back the next day. We hadn't been shopping for a while since we were both going out of town, so I walked to the grocery store that was around the corner from my apartment. It wasn't very far from work, and it was a nice evening. I couldn't shake an uneasy feeling though. I looked around a few times and even stepped in and out of boutiques, pretending to look at things, but I never spotted anyone staring at or following me. It was a strange feeling.

After shopping, I walked home and took the elevator to my floor. My phone had been ringing off the hook, but my hands were full, and I couldn't reach into my purse to answer it. Whoever it was could just leave a voicemail. When I got off the elevator, I found Mike leaning against the door to my apartment.

"Forget how to answer a phone call?" he said.

I glared at him. "No, you ass, my hands are full. A little help?"

He laughed and pulled one of the bags out of my arms.

"What are you doing here?" I asked as we walked into the kitchen.

He set the bag down and started unpacking it. "I just wanted to check in on you and see how the trip went.

Didn't hear from you when you landed, so wanted to make sure you got back okay."

I grabbed all the items he laid out. "Oh yeah, sorry about that. I meant to call you and ended up getting busy and forgot to let you know."

He stared at me for a minute and said, "You? Forget? Who is th—" The doorbell rang before he could finish his sentence.

"You expecting someone?"

I looked at him and shook my head as I walked past him. Before I could get too far, he yanked me back and reached for the 9 mm that he kept on his waistband.

"What are you doing? Why do you need that?"

He turned, looked at me, and shushed me.

What the fuck? We grew up around weapons. Being from Texas, it's weird if you didn't have a gun, but this was unexpected. It was just the fucking doorbell.

Mike looked through the peephole and whispered back to me, "It's a pretty tall guy in a suit. You sure you aren't expecting someone?"

I motioned for him to put the gun away and chill.

He pulled back, but didn't put the gun away.

I opened the door. "Hey, you! What are you doing here?"

James gave me a strange look and then mouthed, "Are you okay?"

I nodded. "Come in. My friend Mike stopped by to see how I was and how the trip went."

By the time I turned around, Mike had holstered his 9 mm and was leaning against the kitchen counter. "Hey, man! I'm Mike."

James didn't let on what he was thinking, but he quickly took Mike's hand to shake it and said, "Nice to meet you. I'm James. I didn't mean to interrupt."

Mike shook his head and said, "No interruption. Christy and I were going to make dinner if you'd like to join us?"

I knew where this was going, and I didn't like it. But it was like a freight train, and I couldn't stop it or look away. I chimed in, "*We?* As in plural? Since when do you cook anything that's not on a grill?"

Mike chuckled. "We just put away some steaks. Figured we could fire up the pit on the roof and have a little cookout. You don't mind, do you, James?"

James looked at Mike, and from their body language, I could tell something was going on, but I didn't want to get in the middle of it. So I said, "Sure, you boys can have the steaks, and I can have a salmon. Mike, why don't you head up and start the pit?"

Mike looked at me, and for a second, I thought he was going to argue, but apparently he thought better of it. He turned around, pulled the things he needed out of the fridge and cabinets, and left.

James and I watched Mike leave and waited until the door was closed before we looked at each other. James arched an eyebrow, but didn't say anything. I laughed.

"What's that look for?"

James didn't respond. He just gave me a pointed look.

"That's my best friend Mike from childhood. We both moved out here after high school to go to Georgetown University. He's the brother I never had. We have been friends for over fifteen years. We can talk about it later. Are you staying over? We can always go to your place if you want."

He didn't respond right away. Eventually, he seemed to come to terms with the situation. "Let's have dinner, and we can head to my place after."

I nodded and gave him a kiss on the cheek before walking to the fridge to grab some drinks.

Dinner with Mike and James was a little…rough, for lack of a better word. Even though he knew Mike was like a brother, James was still a little stiff, and Mike wasn't making it any easier. Neither came straight out and asked each other anything; it was as if they had enough respect for me to silently agree that I was capable of having other male friends.

When it was over, I literally let out a breath of relief. Well, at least "meet the family" was off the list. It could never be any more awkward than it was tonight, and I thanked God for that.

Chapter 11

My alarm rang, and for a minute, I didn't know where I was. It was warm, cozy, and comfortable. I reached to turn off the alarm, and then I realized that James was the reason for the warmth. Thankfully, he hadn't woken up at the sound of my alarm. I watched him for a bit.

He looks so peaceful while he sleeps. He has been amazing to me, and if I'm being completely honest, it scares the shit out of me. I've never had anyone care so much about me the way this man does. Sure, I have Mike, but his love and care is completely different than this. I think I'm falling in love with this man, and there doesn't seem to be anything I can do about it. It's as if my heart and my mind have joined forces and have made their decision. For once, it's not making me feel as though I am having a panic attack or I need to reach for my inhaler.

I watched James for another minute before I kissed his cheek and went off to get ready for work. By the time I was out of the shower, he was dressed and telling me he had a meeting to get to, so he had to run, but he would call me later. I reminded him Annie was coming back today, so I needed to spend some time with her. He kissed me, gave me a little nod, and then he was gone. He left me standing in the bedroom, and for the first time in what felt like a long time, I was truly happy.

Work flew by, and I rushed home as soon as 5:30 p.m. came around. As I charged through the door, I found Annie had just walked in too. I screamed and ran to hug her. I missed her so much. We had been taking these trips for the last couple of years, but somehow this year felt different. She hugged me tight, and when we finally let go, I realized I was crying, and so was she. I let her go get freshened up and unpack while I made dinner.

We sat and ate and talked about our adventures. Apparently, Blake had suggested going on a safari in Africa, and she thought it would be fun. I made a mental note that I needed to figure out what was happening there.

"I missed you so much, Christy! I'm not sure why, but this year feels very different. I feel as if I might not need to do this again. Did you feel that too, or was it just me?" She took a sip of her wine and waited for me to respond.

The crazy thing is, I had felt the same way too. "I felt that way too! When I got home, I felt utterly and completely happy. I'm not sure how or why, but it was like I was truly cleansed this time around."

She looked at me and smiled. We had some light conversation after dinner before we both went off to bed.

The rest of the week flew by. I hadn't seen much of James. Annie and I hit the gym pretty hard. We both felt that we ate too much on our trips. Although a lot of walking had been involved, it didn't help that we'd ingested all the carbs and fat.

When Friday rolled around, I hoped to see James over the weekend. I was just about to text him when Landon walked in and told me Annie was out in the hall and wanted to see about having lunch. I caught the room's attention and told them to take lunch and be back by 1:00 p.m. I thought they deserved an hour and a half for lunch after all the great work they had been doing. I was certain Ana wouldn't mind my making that assumption.

Everyone was so excited they rushed out of the room. I made a quick comment to Landon and asked him to remind me to speak with Ana about this. Then I made my way to the hall.

Annie was beaming. My expression must not have been what she was expecting because her huge smile faltered a bit.

"Hey, sweets! I'm sorry. My morning has been a bit hectic. What's going on? Why are you so happy and excited?"

Her big smile was back, and she was bouncing on both feet. She looped her arm around mine, and we walked toward the elevator as she said, "I am just really excited about this weekend!"

I felt as if I was missing something because I didn't recall making plans with her this weekend.

"Christy! Don't tell me you already forgot! Have you not checked your messages?"

I reached in my purse and found my cell. Lo and behold, there were a few unread messages. I opened them to find it was our group chat. I scrolled up and started from the top. Then it clicked! Mike had told me about this last week and hadn't given me an escape. I looked up, and Annie was staring at me intently, waiting for my response.

"I totally forgot about this weekend."

She laughed and said she thought I had. She's the one who had recommended that we go to Lake Anna.

My head snapped up suddenly.

"Christy, they are going to have to meet sometime. Why not this weekend?"

I could feel the walls closing in, and I had to try to steady my breathing. I knew that I was getting in deep with James, but I wasn't ready to get everyone else involved.

Annie could see I was struggling. When the doors of the elevator opened, she practically dragged me to the outside. There was a light breeze in the air, and it helped steady me. She knew I was having an internal struggle, and she felt it best to just let me figure it out before she pestered me with questions. She led me down the road to our favorite taco place and sat me down at one of the tables before going to the register to place the order.

It wasn't that I wasn't certain James was the one. The problem was that I hadn't even figured out how deeply I felt for him. I had a rule about not bringing anyone around the guys until I was absolutely sure I was ready for a long-term relationship.

Am I there with James? Not to mention the weird dinner with Mike and James. Damn, what am I going to do?

At that moment, Annie reappeared with my drink. "Are you all right now?"

I looked up at her and decided I need to tell her about the awkward dinner with Mike and James. "Yeah, I'm all right. In all the excitement of you coming back, I forgot to tell you about the wonderful dinner I had with my two favorite guys."

She was quiet as she stared out the window for what seemed like a lifetime. "Why would Mikey pull out his gun? That's crazy, isn't it?"

In all the craziness that night, I didn't even ask him about that. I made a mental note to ask him about it the next day. "You know, it was so awkward already that I forgot to even bring it up."

She looked at me and shrugged her shoulders. "Well, if it was that awkward with Mikey, maybe meeting the rest of the clan should wait for some other time. I'm sure you will live if you don't spend every moment of this weekend together. He will understand, you'll see. Talk to him tonight because we leave bright and early tomorrow morning. Hell, why don't you spend the night with him and rush over to the apartment afterward? Mike will be picking us up at 7:00 a.m."

The rest of the afternoon flew by, and at 5:30 p.m., I met Annie in the elevator.

"Hey, sweets!"

I smiled. "Hey, babe, how about we walk home?"

The day was cloudy and breezy. When we reached the apartment, I made my way to the bedroom and sat out on the balcony. Annie came to find me with a bottle of wine. She poured us a glass and sat down. We sat in silence, enjoying the view and the wine. I looked over at her and couldn't help but thank God for putting her in my life.

"Are you going to see James tonight, after all?"

I realized I had not reached out to him at all today and made a run to find my cell.

"Are you all right? I was beginning to worry about you and just called for Nathan to come pick me up so he could take me to your place."

I smiled at the concern in his voice. "I am all right. It's been a long day, and I would love for you to come pick me up." I packed a bag and went back to the balcony to sit with Annie a bit longer.

When the knock on the door came, Annie said she would see me tomorrow and made herself scarce.

"Hey, handsome!"

James gave me a quick once-over before pulling me into a hug and planting a slow but firm kiss on my lips. "Hi, honey."

I slipped out of his embrace and went to grab my overnight bag.

He cocked an eyebrow at the sight of the bag. As he reached for it, he said, "Care to explain?"

I giggled and told him I would explain later.

After telling Nathan to head to the apartment, James closed the window partition. He pulled me onto his lap and started kissing my neck and lightly biting my earlobe.

I sighed and leaned into his kiss.

He stopped. "You need to not make those sounds while we are in public because I won't be able to control myself."

I laughed, gave him a deep kiss, and laid my head on his shoulder. We sat like that the rest of the drive.

He carried me out of the car and up to the penthouse. He didn't set me down until we were inside the apartment. He took my bag to the bedroom, and when he came back, he found me out on the balcony. It was beautiful out there.

He caged me in against the balcony and picked up where he left off in the car. *This man is going to be my undoing.* I was ready for him. Luckily, I had thought about it and had decided to put on a T-shirt dress without panties.

I turned to face him, and we kissed feverishly. My hands made quick work of his belt and jeans. I freed his cock, and he already had pre-cum at the tip. I smeared it around and worked my way up and down his shaft. I knew how good it felt to him because he moaned as he kissed me. I wrapped my legs around his waist, and he lifted my dress to reach for my panties. When he didn't find them, he pulled away slightly and looked at me intently.

"Someone came prepared."

I giggled and guided his cock to my entrance. He started slowly, and it was torture. I needed him. We could get back to slow later, but right now I wanted it fast—if I was being honest, a bit rough too.

As if reading my mind, he wrapped his arms around me to hold me still as he started fast and rough thrusting. The moonlight and the water only intensified the moment, and as I was about to climax, he kissed me to capture my screams.

He wasn't done. He carried me inside to the bed, while his penis was still inside me. The friction was delicious, and I was ready to go again by the time he laid me down. He directed his attention to my breasts, and before I knew it, I was coming again, and he was coming with me. Spent, he lay on top of me, still inside me and semi-erect.

I began to move as I wrapped my arms around him. I didn't want him to go anywhere, and I definitely didn't want him to pull out. He kissed my neck as I ran my nails up and down his back. Apparently, he really liked that because I felt him harden as I kept doing it.

I turned to look at him. "Like that?"

He placed a kiss on my forehead and said, "Mm-hmm."

He started to move slowly, and we went at it for what felt like an hour, just building up the tension. We moved so slowly it was hardly noticeable, but just enough to build the suspense as we kissed. When it finally became too much, I took his hand from my breast and led it to my clit. Together, we rubbed my clit, and then I was lost; he was close behind me. I had never done that with anyone, but with James, I felt safe to explore. The climax must have been too much because I dozed off.

I woke up to find James still lying on top of me. I looked over at the clock on the bedside table and saw it was only 9:30 p.m. The night was young. I felt James's cock twitch. I looked back at him, and he was still asleep. I reached between us and started to rub my clit. I wanted to see if he would waken if he felt me get wet. As I rubbed myself, I began to get wet, and his cock began twitching more frequently. I was watching him intently, and he was still asleep.

But then I felt his hips moving, and he turned to me with a smile on his face. "I love that you are always ready for me."

He pulled out of me, and I whimpered, but he was just repositioning to trace kisses down my body. When he reached the apex of my legs, he took my fingers and licked them before placing his tongue on my clit. He made long swipes from my perineum to my clit and then lightly bit my clit. I let out a scream, and it seemed to encourage him. He blew on it then sucked.

If he kept this up, I wasn't going to last. He must have felt my body tighten because he redirected his tongue to my folds. His did amazing things with his mouth, and I could not hold out. I came in a rush, and it was amazing. He licked me until I was done. Then he put two fingers inside of me and started to tease me into another frenzy. It was incredible.

This time, just as I was going to come, he pulled out his fingers and replaced them with his erection. He did a quick thrust, and I was so full it was painful, but pleasurable. He must have been close because the pace was quick and rough. He kissed me passionately, and then both of us were coming. It was incredible!

After a bit, he got up, and I immediately missed him. To my surprise, he pulled me off the bed and carried me into the bathroom. He set me down on the ledge of the bathtub, turned the water on, and poured in some bath salts.

"I was a bit rough tonight, and I don't want you to be sore. You make me lose my control. Do you want some water?"

I nodded, for fear of speaking, because I knew my voice would break.

Chapter 12

We must have dozed off in the bathtub because, the next thing I knew, my stomach was growling, and we were still in the tub. I nudged James to wake him up and noticed his stomach was growling too. He blinked twice and then realized that we were still in the water. My skin was shriveled up like a prune. I shuddered and stepped out of the bath. I grabbed a towel and tossed it to him while I dried myself and wrapped the towel around me.

My stomach growled again, and James laughed. "Okay, come on. Let's get you fed."

We made grilled-cheese sandwiches and ate them with some chips. We talked about our week, and I finally told him about my weekend plans. I told him we always had a "lake day" to kick off the summer, and that was happening the next day.

He watched me intently and didn't say a word. It almost seemed as if he was upset that I wasn't going to spend the weekend with him. So I let him take the lead, and I stayed quiet. After a little while, he said, "Honey, I am glad you have plans this weekend because I have to go out of town for work, and I didn't know how to tell you. When I saw your overnight bag, I was trying to figure out how to tell you."

I gave him a small smile. "Please don't feel like you can't tell me things. I am a big girl. I can handle being away from you for a few days."

He laughed and said okay. We finished up our food and went to bed.

* * *

I woke up pretty early. I looked over at James, and he was fast asleep. To be honest, I had jitters about everyone meeting each other. I took a shower, got dressed, and headed to the kitchen to make some breakfast. As I was finishing up, I felt a pair of arms wrap around me. I snuggled back into them.

"Good morning, honey. You're up early. Did you sleep all right?"

I looked up at him and smiled. "I slept great! I had a personal heater to keep me cozy all night."

He laughed and kissed my forehead. "What's all this?"

I wriggled out of his arms and showed him what I had been up to. "I have to go because Mike will pick us up at 7:00 a.m., and he's pretty punctual. But I didn't want you to leave without being fed a proper breakfast. I even packed you a snack for the trip."

James gave me one of those lopsided, boyish grins followed by a big kiss. "That was very sweet of you! Thank you!"

I gave him one more kiss and told him I had to go.

"Remember to wear your life jacket before you get out on the water!"

That made my heart warm. "I will! Have safe travels, and let me know when you arrive!"

* * *

The day flew by.

"Hey, kid." I looked up to see Mike sitting next to me.

"Hey, Mikey! Why aren't you out on the water?"

He smiled. "I actually wanted to chat with you."

I sat up and pulled my sunglasses off. "Everything all right?"

"Yeah, everything is fine. I just wanted to talk to you about James."

Oh boy, here we go…

"I noticed you didn't introduce him as your boyfriend the other night. What's up with that?"

I put my sunglasses back on. "It's too soon to call it anything, Mike. We recently started seeing each other, and we haven't really put any labels on it."

He looked out over the water for a bit then leaned back against the railing. "For what it's worth, you seem different…more relaxed. Maybe he's good for you? You seem really happy. Does he treat you well?"

I gave him one of my warmest smiles. "Mikey, if possible, he takes care of and watches over me more than you do. He is amazing. I don't know where this is going, but, honestly, I think he might be the one. I haven't told him as much because I am trying to be a responsible adult about this, but, man, what I feel for him grows daily."

He smiled softly. "I just want what's best for you, Christy. I don't want you to jump all in and get hurt. Try to take things slow. Get to know him. I mean, really know him. Okay?"

It was a little ominous the way he said that, but I tried not to dwell on that. I nodded and kissed his cheek. "Do you think we will be heading in soon? I'm ready for a shower and some real food."

He laughed and said he was ready to call it too.

The guys came back, and we headed back to the lake house we rented. After dinner, we made plans to head back to the city early the next day. Annie and I had planned to walk through a house for Aiden and Lilly. They wanted something close to the university, but not too expensive. Annie and I had scoured the area over the last week, and we narrowed down some places for us to preview. If we deemed them nice enough, we would video chat with Lilly so she could check them out.

The next day, the house hunt was a bust. We ended up calling it quits at around 3:30 p.m.

"Do you think we will ever find something that is close to what Lilly is looking for?"

Annie side-eyed me. "I don't think so. She said that if we can't find something by next week, she is going to book a flight up so she can scour while we are at work."

I couldn't help but laugh at that. "It sounds to me like she just can't wait to come up here again. Hey, should we hit the gym today? What do you think?"

Annie looked a little bashful, and I think I even saw her blush. "I've actually got plans tonight."

I arched an eyebrow. "Is that so?" She was so giddy it was weird. She never acted this way when she was starting relationships. "What gives? Why so cryptic?"

She threw a cushion at me. "Let's see how it goes, and then I will tell you about it. No use in both of us getting our hopes up. Plus, don't you want to see James? He gets home tonight, right?"

My eyes almost bugged out of my sockets. "Shit! I almost forgot! I have to go. I'm going to stay at his place tonight. I'll catch you at the office tomorrow." I jumped off the couch and kissed her forehead before running off to my bedroom to pack. I texted Nate and asked him to pick me up in twenty minutes.

While I was packing, he pinged back and said he was actually around the corner and would be downstairs in less than five minutes. I rushed to pack everything I would need. I didn't want Nate to idle outside for too long.

I called out to Annie that I was leaving and wished her luck on her date before I ran out the door. I spun around so fast after locking the door that I stumbled and started running.

***

"Christy, when are we going to spend some time together?"

That took me by surprise. "What do you mean? Aren't we spending time together now?"

He smirked. "I mean, yes, this is technically us spending time together. But what I mean is *really* spend some time together. Get to know each other."

This was starting to feel more serious than I thought he was willing to be. It seems Mikey had a point about making sure I got to know James better, and now here was my chance. "What did you have in mind?"

He shrugged. "Maybe we can have a little getaway, just the two of us? What do you think?"

I finished packing my bag. "I think that is a good idea, but it would have to be a weekend getaway. I may be able to swing leaving early on a Friday afternoon, but I can't take more time off work right now. Can we start with a weekend?"

He crossed the room and wrapped me up in a hug. "A weekend will be a great start. Come on; let's get going before you get hangry."

I laughed because, in such a short time, he knew me so well.

As we headed back to the city, we talked about what places might be good destinations for a weekend getaway and possible dates for one. We narrowed it down to four places, but had yet to pick one before we parked in front of his apartment building.

I texted Annie to let her know that I was back in the city and that I would meet her at our apartment at 9:00 a.m. the next day. After she confirmed, I tucked my phone in my pocket.

"Everything okay, honey?"

I smiled. I loved when he called me that. "Yes, I was just texting Annie to let her know I would meet her at our apartment at 9:00 a.m. What are we having for dinner?"

He laughed. "I figured you would be starving by the time we got here, so I had Marcus call ahead and have De Mayo's delivered."

My jaw dropped. I had never told him about my infatuation with De Mayo's, and we had never ordered in from there.

He laughed. "I figured you probably worked up an appetite being out on the water all day. I may have cheated and asked Annie what you liked to eat after a day like today."

I couldn't help but hug him tight. It was a small gesture, but it really meant a lot to me that he took such good care of me. When the elevator doors opened, the smell of De Mayo's wafted out, and my mouth watered. We set our bags down and headed for the kitchen.

***

"THAT. WAS. AMAZING." I slouched in my chair while I patted my stomach.

James laughed. "I'm glad we made a good choice. You want to watch a movie?"

I nodded. "You may have to roll me to the living room though."

I was clearly joking, but James didn't take it as such. He walked over to me, picked me up, and walked to the couch. I couldn't help but laugh.

He scowled. "Why are you laughing?"

"I wasn't being literal, you know. I have legs."

He gave me a light kiss. "Why walk when I can carry you."

We snuggled into the couch, and he picked a random movie. I knew I wasn't going to watch it, so I didn't even bother looking at what he was selecting. I sat on his lap with my head on his shoulder, and I couldn't help but think how perfect this was.

Blink. Blink.

I woke up, and it was dark and cold. It was odd because I had fallen asleep on James's lap, warm and cozy. Right now, I was cold and uncomfortable. I looked around and found I was lying up against the couch, and James was nowhere. I heard voices, and I decided to follow the sound. I was barefoot, so I tiptoed toward the sound of James's voice. I don't know why I was sneaking around, but something just felt so odd.

As I rounded the corner, I could hear James speaking to someone, and his tone was curt. He sounded upset.

I stopped there and listened. I knew it was rude, but his tone was very surprising. I mean, I know I didn't know the guy very well, but still it surprised me.

"I don't care what you have to do; just get it done," he growled to someone. "DON'T FUCKING QUESTION ME! When I tell you to do something, you fucking do it. Unless you want to find yourself without a job."

This is crazy! Who the hell is he talking to? Why is he so angry?

He started speaking again, "Don't call me until you have real information to report."

I practically hauled ass to his room and ran into the bathroom. I heard him walk past the bedroom, and I knew he was heading back to the living room. Probably looking for me. I flushed the toilet and began brushing my teeth, so my mouth was occupied when he walked in.

"Hey, honey! When did you wake up?"

I turned to look at him with toothpaste all around my mouth.

He laughed. "I'll wait until you're done." He proceeded to brush his teeth as well.

When we finished, I answered, "Not long ago. I woke up because I was cold and had to pee. I came in here and then realized I should brush my teeth before going back to bed. What were you up to?"

He walked over to me, picked me up, and sat me on the counter. "I had a work call to take care of. I'm sorry you were cold. I can warm you up though." He started kissing me, but I was still thinking about what I heard. He stopped kissing me. "Are you okay? Are you not feeling well?"

I snapped out of it. "Yes, no. I am okay. The counter is just a bit cold, and it's not helping the cause."

He nodded, picked me up, and walked me to the bed. "This should be better."

I thought he would continue his kissing, but to my surprise, he didn't. He tucked me in and climbed over me. When he was settled on his side, he pulled me close and snuggled with me. "Feeling warmer now?"

What a total one-eighty. He was losing his shit on someone not even ten minutes ago, and now he is the gentle lover.

I nodded and turned over. Although I was a little freaked out, I really wanted to see his face to make sure he was still my James. "Much warmer, thanks."

He tucked some of my hair behind my ear and caressed my face.

This is definitely my James.

* * *

I woke up around 6:00 a.m. Not sure why, but I suppose it was because I was well rested since I had taken a nap the previous evening. I looked over, and James was fast asleep. I felt as if I had dreamed the events of last night. There was no way he could be that crazy, angry guy. *Could he?* I shook that thought out of my head.

I decided to watch him sleep for a bit. I did not want to leave this bed or him today, but Annie and I promised we would help Aiden and Lilly. Their moving date was a month away, and none of the houses we had looked at was up to par for them. It was crazy how many requirements they had for the damn house. At this rate, I was going to put them in an apartment with a three-month lease until we could find the perfect house.

As I watched James sleep, I couldn't help but get wet. This man did some crazy things to me. I slowly moved closer to him and found that he was sporting morning wood. He must be dreaming about me. Ha, at least I hoped so. This made my plan a whole lot easier. I slowly and softly startled him and placed his erection at my core. I slowly lowered myself onto him and started moving. It wasn't long before I was dripping wet, and he was blinking his eyes open, a big smile swept across his face.

"Good morning, honey."

His voice was raspy and full of sleep, but it sounded so sultry and seductive that it made me more wet, as if that were even possible. I leaned forward and planted a kiss on him.

He took advantage of the situation and flipped me onto my back and took control. He was soft and gentle at first, but as our hunger grew, the sex became fast and rough. It was exactly what we both needed because I climaxed three times. We went at it for a while, until I realized it was 8:00 a.m. I kissed him and told him I had to start getting ready to go meet Annie.

"Do you really have to go? Why do you have to do the house hunting for your friends?"

I popped my head out of the bathroom. "Because when we were in Miami, I offered, and I am a woman of my word."

Pouting, he said, "What if I get my real estate agent to do all that, and you can stay here with me?"

I walked out of the bathroom and searched for my shoes. "J, I need to do this. My friends are important to me, and I will not be the woman who puts her friends aside just because she is sleeping with someone." I bit my tongue and snapped my head up as I said the last part of that sentence.

He was angry. I could see his jaw tense.

Damn it, Christy! Always putting your foot in your mouth and saying all the wrong things.

"Hey, I'm sorry. We haven't really talked about what"— I motioned with my hand between us—"this is. We picked up and sort of ran with it. Maybe we need to sit down and discuss where we both are and how we want to proceed?"

I could tell he was not very pleased with my suggestion. He got out of bed and began walking away. Before he disappeared into the bathroom, he turned and said, "Okay. Tell me when. Have a good day, and tell Annie I said hello."

As I walked out of the building feeling terrible, Nathan was standing there with a smile on his face and the car door open. I was planning on taking a cab, but it seems even in his disappointment, James wanted to make sure I was taken care of.

"Good morning, Ms. Mills! Where are we off to this fine morning?"

I gave Nathan my best smile. "Good morning, Nate! Is it okay if I call you Nate?"

He let out a low laugh. "It is quite all right, Ms. Mills." He was so sweet. I had never really paid attention, but he was handsome.

No daydreaming, Christy!

"Can we head to my place?"

He smiled and helped me into the SUV. "Of course, Ms. Mills. I am yours for the day." He closed the door as he said that and didn't give me enough time to argue.

When I saw him get into the driver's seat, I asked, "I'm sorry, Nate. I think I misunderstood you. Did you say you were mine for the day? What about James?"

He glanced at me through the rearview mirror. "Mr. Still has instructed me to take you wherever you need to go today. He also made it clear that I should bring you back to his apartment. Whatever time it may be." He said that last line as he blushed and looked away.

For heaven's sake! This man can be positively sweet, but extremely infuriating. I specifically told him that I would see him tomorrow, but he goes and tells Nate to bring me back to his place. Ugh! I really need some girl time.

I texted Annie and told her Nate and I would be down-stairs in about fifteen minutes. She replied quickly and said she would meet us outside. By the time we pulled up, Annie was standing on the curb and looking beautiful in a yellow sundress. I definitely did not get the memo. I was wearing some leggings and a tunic with some Converses. It wasn't a horrible outfit, but it was certainly not as festive as Annie's attire.

Nate pulled up and jumped out of the vehicle to get the door for Annie. "Good morning, Ms. Meyers. How are you today?"

She gave him a megawatt smile and said, "Good morning, Nathan! I am wonderful. How are you today?"

Her mood was infectious. Nathan gave her a big grin. "I am wonderful! Thank you for asking. Shall we?" He motioned to the open car door, and Annie hopped in.

"Good morning, sweets! How are you? What has you in such a great mood? You've even brought out your best sundress!"

She laughed. "Good morning! I just woke up on the right side of the bed, I guess." She gave Nate the address, and we weaved into the morning traffic.

The house was nice. It was a single-story home with an open floor plan. I was not much for stairs. I always felt as if single-story houses were more elegant and allowed for more fluid movement throughout the space, especially when there was an open floor plan. However, we were not shopping for me. We were shopping for Lilly and Aiden.

As the realtor, Lee, went on and on about the house with Annie, I decided to call Lilly. I thought she might want to weigh in on this house because it really was gorgeous, in the neighborhood they were looking for, and in the price range requested.

She answered on the first ring. "Hey, Christy! How's it going?"

I smiled and waved at her. "I am wonderful! Annie seems to be having a good day too! She busted out her supercute yellow sundress."

Lilly started laughing; we knew Annie only wore that dress when she was feeling like a ray of sunshine. Which usually meant she had exciting news.

"Anywho, I called so you could check this house out! I really like it!" I flipped the camera and started walking around.

I could tell Lilly really liked it as well, but the kicker would be Aiden. He was really particular when it came to houses. She called him over, and once more I did a walk-through while Annie had a chat with the realtor. After the tour, both Lilly and Aiden were in love. They asked me to head over to Annie and the realtor, Lee. When I arrived, it seemed as if Annie and the realtor were just finishing up their conversation.

"So what did you think, Ms. Mills?"

I smiled and said, "It doesn't much matter what I think, Lee, but Lilly and Aiden love it! Please say hi." I turned my phone around and flipped the camera so they could see each other.

Annie introduced everyone, and I stepped away for a bit to walk the backyard.

Chapter 13

"Honey, are you okay? You have been a little off today."

I turned to look at Annie. "Hey, I am all right. Just thinking. What did Lilly and Aiden think about the house? Did they like it?"

Annie always knew when I was avoiding talking about something, but she never pushed me. She always gave me the space to try and figure things out on my own. If I couldn't, then she knew I would come to her.

"They actually loved the house. The realtor was drawing up paperwork for them to submit a bid. Hopefully, this is the last house we have to look at," she said with a laugh.

I laughed with her. "Come on; let's go home. I need a shower and some time in my own bed."

As promised, Nate was outside waiting for us. "Where to, ladies?"

Annie turned and looked at me.

For a split second I really almost said home, but I realized I didn't know where that was anymore. This was too much feeling for 11:00 a.m. "How do you feel about brunch?"

Annie's smile was so big; she even almost did a little happy dance.

"Nate, can you take us to Amy's on Fourth?" Annie loved that place. They made the best eggs Benedict.

When we arrived just before the rush, but the place was getting busy. We grabbed a table by the window. After we ordered and the food was delivered, I told Annie about what I had overheard and how out of character it seemed for the James I thought I knew. Then I told her about my slip of the tongue that morning.

Annie looked stunned, and her mouth was in the shape of an *O*. I could tell she was surprised by what I said to James that morning, and she wasn't quite sure what to say. She took a sip of her coffee to try to cover up the shock.

"Christy, I don't understand. I thought you said you were beginning to fall for him. Why would you say 'the guy I'm sleeping with'?"

I just stared at my food to avoid her piercing stare. I gave her a little shrug. I felt small because the fact of the matter was I did, in fact, fall for James, and I was simply pushing him away so I wouldn't get hurt…or, worse, make another mistake so Mikey could add it to the collection. Annie didn't push, but I could tell she was just waiting for a response. I took a few minutes, and then, as always, I admitted what I was feeling to her.

"Oh, honey! It's not like that at all! It's okay to fall for this guy. He isn't like all the other screwups from the past. Plus, you've got your life together. You've got a good job, a place to live, and good people in your life. You are not the same dumb kid you once were. Give yourself more credit than that."

By the end of that, I was crying. *She is right. I can't believe I am avoiding this beautiful, caring man because of my stupid baggage from the past.*

"Annie, do you think I messed things up with James? He did send Nate with me all day and asked him to take me back to his place at the end of the day. Is that a positive sign?"

She patted my hand. "Christy, I think that man is mad about you, and he would do anything to keep you in his life. Give yourself a little grace. You have been through a lot over the years."

I gave her a small smile. "I love you, Annie! I don't think I say that enough. You are the best friend a girl could ask for!"

She smiled while stuffing a piece of bacon in her mouth. "Right back at ya!"

Because of all my drama, I almost forgot about the reason behind her good mood. "Annie?"

She had a huge mouthful of eggs and some yolk dripping down her chin. It was the most carefree I had seen her in a long time. "Yeah?"

I laughed. "What's with the yellow dress? How did your date go last night?"

She chewed especially slowly before taking a sip of her coffee. "Dinner was good," she said as she stuffed more eggs into her mouth.

Oh, this is going to be good. I knew she was hiding something, and I was determined to find out what. "Sweets, you know I will get it out of you. Why are you playing hardball?"

She peered at me, and her shoulders slumped slightly. *That's odd. She's usually excited to talk about her dates.*

"What's going on, Annie? Are you all right?"

She chewed her food for longer than necessary. "I'm all right. I was hoping you would forget about the date though."

That's such an odd thing to say. She knows I usually never forget details like that. I gave her a pointed look and raised an eyebrow.

She let out a sigh. "Christy, its complicated. I am not sure I am ready to discuss it. Do you think you could let this go for a while?"

I had a bad feeling about this. Knowing full well that I would not be able to control my mouth, I simply nodded as a response. She probably knew I wouldn't stay quiet for long, but she seemed to accept my nod anyway. I picked up the check, and we made our way out to Nate.

"How was brunch, ladies?" Nate was standing next to the SUV waiting for us at the curb.

I gave him a winning smile. "It was delicious. Though, I wish you would have joined us like I asked."

His brow furrowed. "As much as I appreciate the offer, Ms. Mills, I don't think Mr. Still would much appreciate me leaving my post."

What an odd thing to say. Surely, James would not be upset if I treated the driver to lunch. Would he? I made a mental note to ask him about it and handed Nate the bag of scones I picked up for him.

"That was too kind of you, Ms. Mills. Thank you very much!"

We got into the SUV and asked Nate to take us to our apartment. Twenty minutes later, we were there, and Mike was outside the building. *Huh, why didn't he call? Did Annie tell him we were heading back?* I quickly discarded that notion because she looked just as surprised to see him. As we pulled up to the curb, I opened the car door and jumped out.

Nate put the car in Park, got out, ran around the vehicle, and shoved me back in the car.

"Hey!" I shouted, but he shut the door before I could say another word.

I looked at Annie in shock, and then we stared out the window. Mike pointed at Nate and signaled that we should leave. Nate ran around the SUV, jumped in, and sped off. Annie and I exchanged worried looks.

I was the one who spoke first. "What the ever-loving fuck was that, Nate!?"

He looked in the rearview mirror multiple times and was very skittish. "I am sorry, Ms. Mills. Slight change of plans. I am to take you to Mr. Still's apartment immediately."

Annie and I exchanged confused looks, and she was the one to speak next. "Nathan, why do I need to go to James's apartment?"

He glanced over his shoulder. "Not my place to say, Ms. Myers. You ladies hang tight. I will have you there in no time, and maybe Mr. Still will have more answers for you both."

I sat back and stared at Annie in shock. *What the hell is going on?*

Fifteen minutes later, we were in the elevator, going up to James's apartment, and being escorted by Nate. The elevator dinged at the penthouse, and as we stepped out, I saw suitcases sitting at the entryway. As I walked by, I realized they were Annie's and mine.

"What the fuck?" Annie seemed just as shocked as I was. "James," I called out.

As we rounded the corner, we could hear him speaking in a very stern tone. "I will have your head if this happens again."

Annie and I stared at Nate, who shook his head. He acted as if this were the most normal thing in the world. As we approached James, he turned around, saw us, and his expression was cautious.

"Hi, ladies, did you have a nice morning?"

Is this guy for real? "Cut the crap, James. What the fuck is going on?" I heard myself say.

His expression hardened for a moment then softened. He walked toward me and reached his hand out for me to take it. I didn't want to, but at the same time, I wanted to feel his warmth. I was so confused and needed answers. I took his hand, and he led us down the hall to his office. He motioned for Annie to take a seat and then pulled me with him to sit at his chair with him. I was so over today that I didn't even fight him.

He was powering up his computer when Mike walked into his office. Annie and I stared at him, completely lost.

Annie was the first to speak. "What the hell? What are you doing here, Mikey?"

He patted her hand and made a head motion toward James.

At this point, the computer came to life. James angled it so we could all see the screen. It had tons of pictures of Annie and me on the screen. They looked like candid shots. *What the hell? How did James get these pictures?* I turned to face him.

He kissed my cheek before answering my unspoken question. "Do you remember what happened the night before you left for Italy?" As I blushed, remembering exactly what happened, James ran his thumb across my cheek. "I didn't like what you told me, and I didn't like the fact that you had someone out there that would possibly want to hurt you. I contacted Mike here and got all the details from him regarding that scumbag."

I gave Mike a pointed look.

James reached out and pulled my chin back toward him with his index finger. "Don't be angry. I needed to know. We can get to those specifics later. I did some digging, and I found out the bastard was up for parole this year."

I froze, paralyzed by fear. *How can he be out already? This is insane! I should have left the city. I should have gone halfway around the world just to get away from him.* I felt James's hand going up and down my back in soothing circles, pulling me back from my spinout.

"Breathe, honey. You are safe. Just breathe."

Mike stood up and got me a glass of water from the bar. "Here, drink this, kid."

I knew I was safe with these two men around, but the fear of that man coming back to finish the job was too overwhelming. I peeked over at Annie, and it looked as if she had seen a ghost. "Annie, are you okay?" My voice was a small whisper.

Mike rushed over to her and pulled her in for a hug. She wept on his shoulder.

I turned back to James. I was still confused as to why he would do this. "James, why did Nate push me back into the SUV and drive off? Why were you at our apartment, Mike? What is going on? And why are Annie's and my bags in your foyer?"

James was still rubbing my back, but Mike was the first to speak. "I was popping in to see you guys and to see if you would be up for brunch. When I got of the elevator,

I noticed your door was ajar. I called the cops and made my way into the apartment. I saw your place was a disaster. The cops came in shortly after I did, and I told them I was the one that called it in. I showed them my key and the pictures of us on the wall. They allowed me to grab some clothes, and I called James. I explained what happened, and he rushed down to check things out.

"When he saw your place, he packed some of your things, and I packed Annie's, and he brought them back here. James was supposed to message Nate before he took you home, but then we noticed the douchebag at the end of the block. The cops started chasing him, and things got out of hand. James took off after him in his car, but ultimately lost him. You all arrived when the chase began, and that's when I told Nate to bring you here."

I turned to look at James.

He nodded. "I won't let anything happen to you. I promise."

Tanner Jenkins. That is the name of the asshole who will forever haunt me. I cannot believe he is out on bail. Much less that he found me and attempted to…what? Finish the job? Why would he even go to my house? I don't understand. Now he's got a warrant out for his arrest because he broke the conditions of his parole. Dumbass. I feel so bad for Annie though. She shouldn't be stuck in this shit. She had nothing to do with it, and now she is stuck here at James's place with us because Tanner fucking Jenkins is out on the loose.

***

I walked out of the bedroom and immediately smelled bacon and waffles. *The girl just went through a shit day, and probably night, but she's out here making me waffles. She deserves a medal and everything good in life.* I walked into the kitchen and saw Annie covered in flour and slaving away at the stove. I wrapped my arms around her and kissed her cheek.

"I love you, but I don't deserve you! Thank you for loving me and never leaving me!"

She turned around and returned my big hug. "Right back at you, sweets! Now, sit down, and let's have breakfast. Does your man eat this kind of food, or do I need to make some of the healthy shit."

Before I could answer—

"I resent that! I eat everything. I am not picky." James harrumphed.

I laughed, and so did Annie.

"Good morning, Annie. Good morning, honey! Did you all sleep well?" James asked while pouring three cups of coffee.

Judging by the stack of waffles on the counter, and all the meal containers on the other end of the island, I knew Annie had not slept a wink. She obsessed by cooking when she was stressed.

I went ahead and answered for the both of us, "It could have been better."

James seemed to understand after he followed my line of sight. "We are going to figure this out, ladies. I want you to know that I have hired a private investigator in addition to working with the police to ensure we catch this scumbag. Annie, these accommodations are temporary, okay?"

She gave him a small smile and nodded. "Are you guys hungry?"

James and I both nodded with big smiles on our faces.

After breakfast, James gave us a lift to the office. He asked us not to leave the building, and he had Nate speak to the head of security to ensure there was no breach and to keep someone near both of us at all times.

"I will bring you ladies lunch, okay?"

We nodded and made our way to the elevator.

"It's going to be okay, Annie. But I am sorry you are being dragged into this nonsense."

She turned and gave me a hug. "You have nothing to apologize for! This is not your fault, and I do not want you blaming yourself for the actions of that douche. Do you hear me!?"

I nodded and sniffled.

The elevator dinged on Annie's floor, and we jumped when Blake and Christopher rushed into the elevator and grabbed us by the arms.

"Oh my God, are you okay?!" they said in unison.

The elevator door closed, and Christopher pushed the twentieth-floor button. When we reached it, they pulled us out of the elevator and into Blake's office.

"What is going on?" Blake asked.

We were confused, so we stayed quiet.

"Annie? Christy?"

I could tell Annie was still reeling, so I took the lead. "What do you mean, Blake?"

He looked at Annie; then his gaze landed on me. "We just received word from our security department that you two are to be guarded by security at all times, and you are not to leave this building. What is the meaning of this? What happened?" He stole another glance at Annie, but I could tell she didn't want to speak.

"It's a bit of a long story." I shrugged.

Christopher spoke this time, "We have time. We had your schedules and our schedules cleared for the morning."

Ah hell...I didn't want to get into this nonsense with our bosses. I wished a way out of this would appear miraculously. But of course it didn't. *Well, here goes nothing.*

"I am awfully sorry that my private life has leaked into our work life. Annie has nothing to do with this, really. She is an unfortunate bystander. When we were in college, we went to a frat party—our first, to be exact—and I wandered off by myself to go to the bathroom. I stumbled into the wrong room and ended up getting sexually assaulted by some guy. Our friends ran in and stopped the guy before he raped me, but I ended up putting him in jail.

"Fast-forward to now—he is on parole. It turns out he has been hunting me, and yesterday he broke into our apartment and ransacked the place. It is an obvious violation of his parole, and there is a warrant for his arrest. People are looking for him, but he has been evading the police. It is suspected that he will try to find me again and come after me…or Annie by association. Thus, we are to be watched or escorted at all times."

I blushed and looked down at my feet, embarrassed about all this, when I noticed Christopher kneeling down in front of me.

"Christy, I am so sorry you went through that awful experience. We didn't mean to pry; we were just concerned. When James messaged us to keep an eye on you both, we thought the worst. Thank you for trusting us and telling us what happened. There is nothing to be embarrassed about. We will make sure you are well taken care of while you are here at work. We assume James is taking care of the rest of the time."

I nodded, and I could hear Annie sniffling. I saw Blake pick her up and wrap her in his arms. Annie melted and cried on his shoulder.

After that, the workday seemed to whirl by. Close to five o'clock, I saw Christopher heading in my direction.

"Hi, Christy, how's the day going?"

I saved the document I was working on and closed my laptop. "Hi, Christopher, the day is going all right. The team is progressing nicely with all the accounts we have, and we are almost done with Mr. Still's account. What's going on?"

He scratched the back of his neck. "Nothing. Why do you ask?"

I smirked and tilted my head sideways. "Really, Christopher? You mean to tell me you came down here to just ask how things are going? You usually send an email for that. Why are you really down here?"

He walked in, closed the door, and took a seat. "Christy, I am concerned about you. While I know you are safe in the office, I don't think it's a good idea for you to work from the office right now. I think it's best that you work from home for a while. Security has been on edge all day, and they have been struggling to maintain their normal routine because they are all trying to ensure that no one enters the building without proper identification and without appointments. I want what is best for you, and at this point in time, we think it best that you work from home. Blake and I will ensure that everything is set up for you to be comfortable working at home." He rubbed his hands together and sat, nervously waiting for my response.

"Christopher, I am truly sorry to be such a burden. I never imagined this man would seek revenge. I hate to be putting you all through this, and I really appreciate all you are doing to help keep me safe and, of course, all of the accommodations you are willing to make for me. I'm surprised Blake isn't here with you. You two usually handle difficult situations together."

He chuckled. "Um…Blake is actually giving the same speech to Annie…with some mild modifications, of course."

My eyebrows shot up, and for the first time, I realized Blake was really into Annie, and the feeling was mutual. "OMG!" I looked over at the door to ensure it was shut. "Are you telling me that Blake and Annie…? Are they…? OMG! Is that why…? No? Really?" I couldn't finish a single sentence.

Christopher was in full-out laughter mode now. "Settle down, Christy. I believe they are, and it seems they both are happy about it. He will actually be taking you and Annie back to James's house tonight. I am sure Annie will explain everything then. Are you ready to go? I will have Landon take everything to you at James's house."

Oh, I nearly forgot about Landon! "Christopher, how will this arrangement affect Landon? He is an excellent employee!"

He smiled softly. "Don't worry, Christy. Landon's job is safe. He will actually have a hybrid position now. He will spend most days with you at your home office, and the rest of the time, he will be going back and forth between the office and James's to ensure anything you and the team need to exchange physically gets handled."

I let out a breath I hadn't realized I was holding. "Oh, thank goodness! I can't imagine life without Landon!"

Christopher laughed. "Don't worry. Now, come on; let's get you home."

We met Annie and Blake on the eighteenth floor. "Christy!" Annie screeched and rushed into the elevator to greet me. "Did Christopher tell you?"

I pulled back and waggled my eyebrows. "Something to tell me?"

She laughed and smacked my shoulder. "You are impossible. Come on; let's go."

Blake had a car waiting at the curb in front of the office. As we were making our way to the front doors, we heard a loud bang, and people started screaming. Christopher pushed me to the floor as he landed on top of me, while Blake did the same with Annie.

I looked frantically over at Annie, and I saw the fear in her eyes. Security ran around closing doors and looking for the source of the obvious gunshot.

"CHRISTY!!!" Annie screamed, and I saw her push Blake off her as she rushed toward me. She shoved Christopher away, and I yelled as she grabbed my leg. I looked down and saw Annie's hands soaked in my blood. "Belt! Wrap the belt above the source!"

I was starting to feel woozy. Blake stripped his belt off while Christopher propped me up against his chest so I wouldn't pass out. Annie was screaming, and the last thing I heard before everything went black was the ambulance.

Chapter 14

"Argh." I blinked a few times; the too-bright lights were not helping my headache. *What the hell? Tanner fucking Jenkins has lost his marbles! I can't believe he seriously shot me!* I didn't know it was him, for sure, but I felt it must have been.

"Christy?"

I blinked a few times more and attempted to fully open my eyes again. This time, I saw Annie's sad, watery eyes staring at me.

"Oh my God, Christy! Sweets, I am so glad you are okay! I am so upset I could kill that bastard!"

That got my attention. I snapped my head toward her. "What bastard? What the hell happened? Where am I?"

Just then, the door burst open, and James ran in. "Honey! Are you okay? I got here as fast as I could!"

I turned to look at him, and he looked awful. I blinked a few more times just to make sure I wasn't imagining it, but nope. He did look awful! "J, are you okay?"

He straight-out started laughing. "Are you joking, love? You are the one that gets shot, and you are asking me if I am okay? The question is, are you okay?"

I nodded. "Yes, I am okay. Honestly. I can't even feel it."

The door swung open, and a man wearing scrubs walked in; he had a kind face. "That is because you are still anesthetized. Good morning, Christy! I am glad you are awake now. You gave us quite a scare last night. Did Annie here explain what happened?"

I shook my head. "No, not yet. I just woke up." I blinked a couple of times.

"Well then, it is nice to meet you! I am Dr. Singh. I am the orthopedic surgeon who performed your surgery last night. I gather you know you were shot?"

I nodded.

"Well, the bullet nicked your femoral artery. I and a vascular surgeon, Dr. Jones—who will probably come in later to see you—repaired the artery, and I had to place an intramedullary nail to stabilize your femur. Do you mind if I take a look? Would you like them to step outside?" Dr. Singh specifically glanced at James.

I smiled. "It's a pleasure to meet you, Dr. Singh! Thank you so much for saving my life! Please proceed. Annie and James can stay. They are my family." I didn't miss the smile that broke out across James's face.

Dr. Singh pulled off my blanket and began peeling the bandages. Once he had removed all the dressings, I heard James gasp.

I looked at him and noticed he had a pained expression on his face. I gave him a small smile and turned back to Dr. Singh. "How's it looking, Doc?"

He looked up at me and smiled. "It's looking good! I would like to keep you a few more days. I am certain Dr. Jones would agree, but he will have the final say. Physical therapy will be by later today to get you started. I expect you should be able to get back on your feet in a couple of weeks. However, it will be with crutches. Do you have stairs in your home?"

I shook my head.

"Good, you won't be able to do those just yet. I will be by again tomorrow. Let me know if you have any questions."

I smiled at him. "Thank you, Dr. Singh! I will see you tomorrow."

As soon as the doctor left, James walked over to me and placed a kiss on my forehead. "I am so sorry I wasn't able to get here before now. I had to fly out to Miami yesterday to handle some business, and I was stuck out there until this morning. I was losing my mind when Christopher called and told me you got shot. I was frantic and spent hours at the airport trying to persuade people to give up their seats so I could get here sooner. I almost booked a car, but an old woman offered to give up her seat."

I gawked at him. "James, you didn't have to rush like that. I'm sure Annie relayed that I was fine, didn't she?" I looked over at Annie.

"Of course, I did, Christy." She looked offended.

"She did, but I couldn't let you lie here alone. I needed to make sure I was here for you. I should have told you I was heading out, and should have made you come with me. It was stupid, and it won't happen again."

I shook my head. "J, chill out. I'm all right. You don't have to blame yourself like that! I am certain I wasn't alone. Right, Annie?"

She smiled and nodded. "I haven't left your side. Well, except while you were in surgery. Blake took me to James's house to pick up essentials for me and you and brought me back. He is still here in the waiting room. He refuses to leave. Christopher had to go hold down the fort, but he is traumatized, for sure. The bullet grazed him before hitting you. Tanner fucking Jenkins is a waste of space and should be put down." She was fuming, and I didn't miss the way James's neck was straining from the pressure of his clenched jaw.

"Do we know it was him?" I asked.

She turned and looked at James, who had a grim expression on his face.

"James?"

He looked down at me. "One of my security guys found his nest, got the security footage from the building he was in, and found out it was him. We turned it over to the authorities, and he is now wanted for attempted murder."

I gasped, and tears welled up in my eyes. "Murder?" I looked from James to Annie.

"Oh, honey, I am sorry. I shouldn't have said that to you just now. We aren't certain he was aiming to kill you, but the simple fact is, you don't really shoot people to injure them. Don't cry, honey. I am sorry."

Annie came nearer to hold my hand. "Sweets, don't cry. He didn't mean to upset you. That piece of shit is not worth your tears!"

I couldn't understand why Tanner Jenkins couldn't just accept the consequences of his actions and move on with his life. Why did he have to come after me? *What a piece of shit! I could kill him!*

A knock on the door pulled me from my thoughts. I looked up to see Blake walking in with some coffee and food.

"Christy! Thank God, you are awake! We were so worried! Annie and I took turns sleeping last night while watching over you."

I smiled at him with fresh tears slipping from my eyes. "Aw, thank you so much, Blake! I truly cannot express how thankful I am! How is Christopher? I would like to video chat with him if possible. OH MY GOD, Annie! Did you call Mikey???"

She squeezed my hand. "Yes, sweets. He is out in the waiting room."

Blake cleared his throat. "Actually, I would like to take Annie home so she can shower and get some rest. They only let two people in at a time, but I told them I would only be dropping off food. Mike said he would come in when Annie steps out."

Annie was about to protest—I could tell—but I squeezed her hand. "Annie, it's okay. Go take a shower. Change your clothes. Make some waffles. I will be okay."

She leaned down and kissed my forehead. "I will be back in a couple of hours. I love you! James, I will get you some fresh clothes. Do you need anything else?"

He smiled and shook his head. "No, thank you, Annie. I greatly appreciate it! Be careful. Do not leave Blake's side!"

She nodded, and Blake snapped his jaw shut. A move that didn't go unnoticed.

"I will make sure Annie is safe!" Blake promised me.

I nodded to him, and they stepped out.

James looked at me and was about to say something when Mike walked into the room. He rushed over to me and kissed my forehead. "Jesus, Christy! You scared the shit out of me! I spent all night looking for that piece of shit with James's security guys. Are you okay? What did the doctor say?" He looked from me to James.

I reached for Mike's hand and squeezed it. "I am okay. The doctor said I should be up and walking around soon. They will keep me here for a few days. Did you really spend all night looking for that lunatic?"

He squeezed my hand back. "Of course, I did. He will not get away with this. Mark my words. Between James's security, me, and the police, we will find this scumbag. I'm going to head out because I have to go to work, but I will swing by later today. Okay? Love you!"

I smiled at him. "Love you too!"

He kissed my cheek and squeezed my hand before he left.

I watched as Mike walked out, and then I turned to look at James. I tried to scoot to the side of the bed. When I failed, James looked at me with curious eyes. "I was trying to scoot over so you could sit next to me." I frowned.

James chuckled. He grabbed the sheet that was under me and pulled on it, which caused me to move closer to the edge of the bed. He then walked around to my uninjured side and sat next to me. "Is that what you wanted?"

I smiled up at him and snuggled into his side. "Yes, exactly what I wanted! I missed you. I was really scared."

He put his arm around me and kissed the top of my head. "I missed you too, love. I was terrified when Christopher called me," he admitted.

I popped my head back up. "Could you call Christopher so I can video chat with him?"

He nodded and fished his phone from his pocket. A couple of rings later and Christopher appeared on the screen.

"Christopher!" I exclaimed. "Oh my God! Thank you for trying to cover me when the shot rang out! Annie told me the bullet grazed you! Did you get it looked at? Are you all right?"

He chuckled. "Christy, sweetheart, I believe the question is, are *you* all right?" I am fine; it was just a scratch. I am sorry I couldn't be there today. As you can imagine, there was a lot of chaos after the bullet broke the glass in the lobby. Since Blake didn't want to leave Annie's side, it only made sense for me to come handle everything over here. I hope you know that my thoughts and prayers are with you, and I will swing by later today. Okay?"

I smiled. "I am so glad you are all right! I was so worried when Annie told me you were hurt! I am so sorry about all of this mess! Please forgive me."

He shook his head. "Nothing to forgive! Work on getting better! I'll come see you later! Try to get some rest! I have got to run."

I nodded, and he hung up. I looked up at James and snuggled against him again.

* * *

I must have fallen asleep because when I opened my eyes, I was back in the middle of the bed, and James was sitting on the chair next to me. "Hey, when did you move?"

He looked up at me with a sour look on his face. "About an hour ago. The nurse said it was not in your best interest for you to be so close to the edge of the bed. She shooed me off the bed and pulled you back to the middle. I am glad you are up because physical therapy will be here in ten minutes."

I grimaced. "I am not sure I'm ready for that."

He smiled at me. "I am going to help you get through this, you know."

I nodded, reached for his hand, and gave it a firm squeeze. I couldn't get the words out to tell him how much it meant to me that he was here and that he wasn't going anywhere.

Dr. Jones came by and said he wanted to keep me in the hospital for a few more days, but I should be able to get around on crutches. He told me to take it easy, and James assured him that I wouldn't need for anything. Dr. Jones smirked at him and winked at me.

The rest of the week flew by, and by Saturday, I was being discharged. Everyone was at the hospital. There were so many security guards around that it looked as if a damn celebrity were being discharged. James was really going overboard, and Mikey was right there with him.

We made it to James's house without incident. Annie and Blake were there with Christopher; they had balloons and cake as if it was some sort of party.

"AHHH! You're home! I am so glad you are finally out of the hospital!" Annie squealed as she wrapped me up in a hug. Blake and Christopher came from behind her and hugged me until James and Mikey broke it up and pulled me over to the couch.

"That's enough of standing for one day. Christy needs her rest," James said as he pulled me onto his lap.

I glared at him and turned to see everyone watching. They all burst out laughing while James harrumphed behind me.

"Don't mind him, guys. He's a little grumpy today. Thank you for being here. Is that cake I see over there?"

"It sure is, and it's your favorite!" Annie exclaimed as she clapped and ran to grab the cake; Blake brought up the rear with the plates, forks, and a knife. Annie cut some pieces of cake and passed them around, while Mikey walked over to the bar and got drinks for everyone except me.

I frowned. "What about me?"

He chuckled, and James kissed my neck. "You cannot have any liquor while on pain meds, honey."

I pouted as I took another bite of cake.

"Don't pout, sweets! I got you some chocolate milk. Here," Annie said.

I grinned from ear to ear. "Thanks, love! You always have my back!"

The rest of the afternoon went by pretty quickly. I hadn't realized how late it was until I started yawning. I looked at James's watch and saw it was almost 9:00 p.m. I looked over at James, and he got the hint.

He stood up with me in his arms, turned around, and told everyone we were going to bed. He suggested everyone pick a guest room because they were welcome to stay. I said good night to everyone, but Annie followed us upstairs. When we got to the bedroom, James raised an eyebrow at Annie.

She put her hands on her hips. "You cannot expect me to trust you to be able to help her shower and get ready for bed by yourself."

I wonder if James is scared of Annie; he didn't argue much.

It took some time to figure out how to cover my injuries, and it took some fancy footwork by James to figure out the best way to hold me so Annie could help scrub me down. The whole thing was completely embarrassing.

"Can we maybe not do this again? I mean, I love you, Annie, but really? You're just scrubbing everything, and—"

She tsked. "Chill out, Christy. It's nothing I haven't seen before. You need to be clean to avoid infections, and it was a bit short notice to get a night nurse out here for the weekend. James and I will take care of this for the weekend, and by Monday, James will have someone out here who may be able to get you squared away with sponge baths."

It took some time to get through my nightly routine, but thankfully we completed it with only a few scrapes and bruises. When I finally got to lie down, Annie gave me a big hug and whispered, "If you need anything that you can't ask James for, shoot me a text, okay?"

I nodded and kissed her cheek. "Goodnight, love! Thank you for everything!"

She kissed my cheek and walked out of the bedroom after tossing a good-night to James over her shoulder.

James walked out of the closet in his sweats and yelled, "Night, Annie," to a closed door. He walked over to my side of the bed and pulled the covers over me. I watched as he poured me a glass of water and plugged my phone into its charger. He also walked over to my backpack and pulled out my glasses and my book, then placed them on the nightstand. He turned the lights out, walked over to his side of the bed, and jumped in.

It's weird how, in such a short time, he already knows my nighttime routine and where I keep all of my things.

I reached over and flicked off my bedside lamp. As I nestled back under the covers, I felt James pull me against him.

"I missed being able to sleep next to you," he whispered.

I turned slightly to look at him, and the smile on his face melted my heart. I kissed him on the cheek and grabbed his hand, which was lying on my stomach. "I missed sleeping next to you too! J, just be careful with my leg, okay?"

That was probably the worst thing to say because he moved away from me and started fussing. "Are you okay? Did I hurt you? Do you need painkillers?"

I pulled him back against me before he jumped out of bed. "I am okay, J. I just worry about sleeping. What if I forget and hurt myself when I turn over?"

He wrapped his arms around me and kissed my neck. "You will not hurt yourself. I will make sure you get your rest without doing anything to hurt yourself. Okay? Get some sleep. I will keep watch for a while. I won't nod off until I feel you are in a deep sleep."

Chapter 15

Six months later…

"Argh, I am so over Tanner Jenkins and the fact that he is still on the loose!!!!"

Annie stared at me with her arms crossed. "Christy, you have to stop! It is not healthy; this obsession you have of finding Tanner Jenkins is not going to end well. You need to let it go. Let the professionals handle it."

The thing is, I want to. I want to let it go and leave it to the cops to find him, but at the same time, I know this cretin will linger in our lives until he is dead, or I am. And the truth is, I am so tired of James, Annie, Mikey, and everyone else walking on eggshells around me for fear I may fall apart at any moment.

It's been six months, and I have just finished my physical therapy. The therapist thinks I am doing excellently and thinks the doctor will give me a clean bill of health on Friday, but I cannot enjoy this moment because ultimately I know that waste of space is still wandering the streets, just waiting to get a second chance at me.

Everyone is so paranoid that they won't let me out of this building. James is so damn rich he literally had a physical-therapy gym installed in his existing gym. I haven't had fresh air in six months. It's unbelievable and so incredible frustrating. I have been looking at, reading, and rereading all of the files, pictures, and reports that the police send over, trying to see if I can find a clue as to where Jenkins might be. I am currently doing that, which is why Annie is so upset.

"Okay, Annie, I will lay off looking for this asshat."

She knows I am placating her, but she accepts it anyway.

James is driving me insane! He won't let me out of the house, and he won't leave my side. In the last six months, every meeting he had has either been held here in the penthouse or rescheduled at some time in the future tentatively.

I called Blake and Christopher last week while James was in one of those meetings, and I actually convinced them to let me come into the office, so I can stop working remotely. After much negotiation, they only agreed if James was on board. I told them it wouldn't be a problem, but I asked them to let me talk to him before they said anything. The deal was that I could return to work at the beginning of the next month. That gave me a solid three weeks to work on getting James on board. Now the real challenge begins...

Over the course of the last week I have strategized on how to pull this off. Blake and Christopher made it very clear that if James even hesitated, I would remain a remote employee until the Tanner Jenkins situation was resolved. After mentally going back and forth on how I can persuade James to get on board, I decided that, as a CEO, he would appreciate a good plan, so I drafted one:

Step 1: Buy Kevlar vest and backpack

Step 2: Agree to be dropped off and picked up

Step 3: Eat lunch in the building — No outside lunch plans

Step 4: Use bodyguards

Step 5: Take self-defense classes

Seems like a pretty solid plan. I just need to organize everything and then sit and speak with James. I think this could work!

"HAVE YOU LOST YOU GODDAMN MIND?!?! ABSOLUTELY NOT!" James yelled.

I shrugged and sat on the coffee table, waiting for him to calm down. As I watched him pace up and down the length of the living room, I prepared my next statement. I had to pack a punch. So far, all I was able to get out of my mouth before he went apeshit was, "I want to discuss me returning to the office." That was all it took for him to blow up. So now, here I sit, waiting for his ears to stop fuming black smoke and the vein on his forehead to stop bulging so that I can proceed with laying out my five-step plan.

After what seemed like hours, James finally calmed down and sat across from me on the couch. He stared at me for a bit before he leaned forward and took hold of my hands. "Christy, I understand the last six months have been torture for you. I understand that you feel trapped, and you just want to be free. But can you understand why I cannot agree to you returning to work at the office? That was where he got to you. He probably did deep research on your office and probably knows every nook and cranny of that place. I do not feel comfortable with you returning to the office."

I sat silently for a moment. I wanted James to know that I really was listening to what he was saying and that I was processing it. This was not something that I was taking lightly, by any means. As I took time to really let his words sink in, he just sat there and stared at me. Allowing me time.

I can honestly say that in such a short time, I have grown to love this man. The way he loves me and cares for me is intense and all-consuming, but I need him to know that I am capable of handling myself as well. I am not going to sit here and act like a victim all my life.

So I took a deep breath and dove in, "James, I hear you. I understand every sentiment you have expressed. I have thought the same way you have about this situation and the very possibility that Jenkins could get to me at the office. However, I also know that he caught me off guard before. I didn't know he was being released. I cannot sit here and wonder if, had I known, things would have turned out differently.

"What I do know is that I am better now. I have recovered from the injury, and I am even more mentally prepared for dealing with this swine. I just need you to trust me. I have been thinking about this for a long time now. This is not a decision I made lightly, and I considered every aspect. I have a plan. Will you let me share it with you?"

He sat there for a few minutes and just stared at me. He slowly let go of my hands and leaned back against the back of the couch. He rubbed his temples—something, I had come to realize, he did when I irritated him, and he was trying to calm down before he spoke to me. I let him soak all that in while I remained silent.

"You aren't going to let this go, are you?"

I gave him my best doe eyes and shook my head.

He sighed and said, "Okay, I will hear you out, but I am not agreeing to anything yet."

I gave him a small smile. "Okay, wait here. I'll be right back!" I jumped up, ran down the hall to the foyer closet, and pulled out the boxes with the Kevlar. I carried them back to the coffee table and set them down.

James's eyes bugged out when he saw the Kevlar logo. "What the hell is this?"

I shushed him and told him this was part of my five-step plan. I pulled out the vest and the backpack. "Okay, so like I said, I have a five-step plan. I know there are some things that I might not have thought of, and that may be something to discuss, but please have an open mind."

He nodded.

I laid out my entire plan, and he did not interrupt me as I spoke to each point. Once I was done, he just sat there inspecting the Kevlar backpack. I wanted to ask him his thoughts, but I was scared he would freak out and be pushed to say no again. So I just sat there in front of him and waited.

The silence was deafening, but there was a bit of a reprieve when the doorbell rang.

I looked over at the television screen, and it showed that Mikey was at the door with pizza. I looked over at James; he was still staring at the Kevlar backpack. I stood up and went to let Mikey in.

"Hey, Mikey! Is it pizza night already?"

He laughed and gave me a kiss on the cheek. "Yes, it is! Are we setting up in the kitchen or the living room?" he asked as he turned and walked into the living room. He saw James sitting there with a backpack in his lap, so Mikey walked over to the coffee table and set down the pizza. "What's with the backpack, J? You taking a trip somewhere?" As Mikey looked up, he noticed the Kevlar boxes and the vest. He jerked his head toward me. "Explain NOW!"

I went through the whole plan again while James sat there. Not a single word had come out of his mouth since before I told him the plan.

Now, Mikey knew the plan, and he straight-up lost it. "NO, THE FUCK YOU ARE NOT GOING BACK TO THE OFFICE! HAVE YOU FORGOTTEN THERE IS A NUT-CASE ON THE LOOSE CHASING YOU?!?"

I shook my head and pointed at the Kevlar. I knew there was no point in saying anything to Mikey when he was this agitated.

"CHRISTY! YOU CAN'T BE SERIOUS!" He looked at James, waiting for him to back him up, but James was still sitting there silently. "JAMES! ARE YOU REALLY GOING TO JUST SIT THERE?!"

This was when James reacted. "Mike, lower your voice. Shouting isn't going to get us anywhere. I have voiced my concerns as well and the reasons why I think this is a ter-rible idea. And while I wholeheartedly agree with you on this, ultimately it is Christy's decision. I cannot make her doing anything. I have done everything I can over the last six months to keep her safe and away from the world, but if she chooses to reclaim her life, I cannot stop her. The best I can do is support her and provide her with all of the assistance she will require to be safe."

I looked back and forth between them as they just stared at each other. It was as if they were having a silent conver-sation that I could not decipher. So again I sat there and waited. It seemed to take ages for their silent conversation to conclude.

Mikey spoke again, "Fine. But I will be the one to handle the self-defense classes. I know a guy, and he's the best."

I was in shock, but mostly excited about the prospect of leaving the house! I ran to Mikey and gave him a big hug. Then I ran to James, jumped on his lap, and kissed him!

Mikey mumbled something and walked off, heading for the kitchen.

James pulled away from the kiss and looked me in the eyes. "Me agreeing to this does not mean that I will stop doing everything in my power to protect you. If I feel it is unsafe to go to work one day, you will not go. Your safety is our number one priority. Do you understand?"

I nodded and kissed him again.

***

One week later, James arranged for my drop-off at work. He insisted on riding along. I didn't fight him. I understood his apprehension, and if I was being honest, I was pretty on edge too. The Kevlar vest was so damn heavy even though I had bought the light one. My guess is it would take some time to get used to wearing it and the backpack.

We rode to the office in silence. There wasn't much to say on the rainy morning. It was as if the weather had spoken for us. As we approached the building, I readied my backpack, but when I looked back up, I saw we were driving past the building.

"James, where are we going?"

He looked at me confusedly. "We are dropping you off at work."

I looked at him while pointing toward the back of the SUV.

He chuckled. "You didn't think we would drop you off at the front of the building? Christy, that's where he got to you last time. Blake and Christopher had a private entrance installed to ensure your safety. The project was initiated the day after you were shot."

I stared at him in disbelief. I had no words. This was next-level paranoia, but I suppose it was prudent to be extra cautious.

As we turned into the parking garage, we entered a sealed tunnel that opened as we approached. It was high-tech shit. Like something out of a movie. They had spared no expense. When we exited the car, James walked me to the elevator and rode up with me to my floor. When we exited the elevator upstairs, Blake and Christopher were waiting.

"Christy!" they yelled in unison.

I walked forward and gave them each a hug. "Hey, Blake! Hey, Christopher! How are you both?"

They each gave me a tight squeeze and said hello to James. We walked to my office. When we entered, they gave me a tour of the changes they had implemented in my absence—bulletproof glass walls, bulletproof desk, panic room, and panic buttons. It was overwhelming, to say the least.

"Blake…Christopher…this…this is…too much," I said, crying at this point.

They shook their heads, and Christopher spoke first. "Christy, the day we got shot was the scariest day of my life. I say that not because I got shot, but because I was unable to protect my best friend's love of his life. There is nothing I won't do to ensure that never happens again."

I was speechless.

Blake took this opportunity to speak. "Christy, you are part of our family now, and there is nothing we wouldn't do for the people we love."

I cried. I stood there and cried.

They took turns hugging me and then made their way out of my office to give James and me some privacy.

When I was able to control myself, I looked up at James. "Did you know they did this?"

He nodded.

Christopher's words were running around in my head—*"best friend's love of his life."* James had not literally told me he loved me, but I knew he cared about me. I couldn't help myself; I had to find out. "About what Christopher said—"

Before I could finish my question, James cut in. "He speaks truth, but that will not be the way I first say it, so let's table that conversation. Okay?" I just looked at him as he leaned down, kissed my forehead then my lips, and said, "Have a great day! I will be back to pick you up at 5:00 p.m."

Chapter 16

It has been three weeks since I started going back to work at the office; James and I are finally getting into a routine. James can't always ride along with me. Even though I told him that I don't need him to join me since he is paying for a bodyguard, he insists that either he or Mikey accompany me on these drives.

So, of course, I took advantage of the situation when James told me Mikey would be the one riding with me to work. "Mikey, please! You know, if you don't help me, I'm just going to figure out a way to do it myself." I pouted as I crossed my arms.

He paced the length of my office, clearly upset at himself for even coming here in the first place. "I want the record to show that I am only doing this because you're a stubborn ass who will get yourself killed by being reckless."

I did my best to stifle a smile. "Noted."

A few days later, Mike dropped by the office at 3:45 p.m. "Come on; get your things. We need to leave. I sent a message to James that I would be picking you up after work so we could get another workout session in before the weekend. He didn't see the need for adding another workout session and said he would pick you up today."

I jumped out of my chair immediately and called Landon into my office. "Landon, please forward my calls to my cell phone. I will be heading out early today. If you need anything, you can reach me on my cell phone. If Blake or Christopher ask where I have run off to, just let them know I had a self-defense class that I forgot I had scheduled. If James happens to come by or calls, just let him know the same."

"You remember my friend Mike? He will be escorting me to the class."

Mike waved at him, and Landon set off for his desk.

Thirty minutes later, we arrived at the DC Metro Gun Range. Mike had a collection of handguns, and he brought a few with him so I could test them out. I was a pretty good shot with rifles, but handguns were still hit or miss. Mikey had a derringer, a Beretta, a .45 Colt, a Desert Eagle, and a GLOCK 19.

We opted to begin with the derringer—a small handgun with a nice handle, but the problem is it only carries one bullet in its chamber. It is not the most efficient of weapons, but I could not say any of this out loud. I could not risk giving away my plans to Mikey. So I picked it out and did my best to aim and reload quickly. It was not my favorite, and it showed on the target.

Next, we moved on to the revolver; this one was better, but it was a bit heavy. I did better with the target on this one.

But Mikey was not pleased. "You're shit at this. It shouldn't be this hard. You are a good shot with rifles and shotguns. This is too much of a variance. Are you doing it on purpose?" He stared at me as if he were looking into my soul. "Christy, I swear, if you are up to something, I will find out. Out with it!"

I looked at him with what I hoped was a shocked expression. "What are you going on about, Mikey? I am just rusty. I haven't shot a gun in ages. You know that. You know exactly the last time I used a gun, and I haven't picked one up since." It was a low blow, but I hoped using that memory would get him off my back so we could continue with the lessons. I felt awful about doing that, but it got the point across, and we continued on with the lessons.

As we made our way through his inventory, I became a better shot, and he eventually agreed that I was in fact rusty and just needed to get warmed up. He said, moving forward, we would only practice with a 9 mm. While the .45 was okay, it seemed to be a bit too heavy. After about an hour, we gathered our stuff and headed out.

"Why are we going to the gym?"

He deadpanned, "We were supposed to be working out, remember?"

Oh shit, that's true.

Thankfully, Mikey had my gym bag in the back of his car. We got a quick HIIT workout in and then headed back to the penthouse.

When the elevator opened, a furious James was standing in the hall. I ran out and jumped toward him, and he opened his arms just in time to catch me. I felt him relax, but only slightly. I kissed his cheek. "Hey! How was your day?"

He set me down and stared at me for a bit; then he looked at Mikey who was still in the elevator, holding the door open. "Mike, will you be joining us for dinner?"

Mikey, probably picking up on the tone of James's voice, decided he was going to go. He waved goodbye and let the elevator door close.

James turned to me and saw me struggling with all my bags and trying to kick off my shoes. He helped me remove a shoe and then jumped right in. "Why did you two need another workout session this week?"

I looked up at him. "Because I didn't do that great in my last session, and Mikey was not pleased. He said I had to get these moves down so we could move forward."

James grabbed my bags and walked behind me toward the bedroom. "I don't understand why you feel the need to get so much self-defense training in. That coward is not going to come anywhere near you. He will most likely do his bidding, much like last time, from afar."

I turned to look at James. "I understand that you don't like it when I am out of your sight, but honestly, James, you really need to quit this caveman bullshit. I am a grown woman capable of caring for myself. While I appreciate the love and care that you shower on me, it does not mean that you will be by my side every second of every day. I need to be able to take care of myself and fend for myself in situations where none of you are present. Surely, you can understand this."

His expression softened. "I do understand, Christy. I just…" He struggled with the words and ran a hand through his hair.

I crossed my arms and stared at him with annoyance. "JUST WHAT, JAMES?"

He turned and looked at me with warm brown eyes. "I love you, Christy."

It was said so softly that I almost missed it through my rising anger. And then I realized that while James and I expressed a lot of other emotions, we had not said those words to each other.

I relaxed my stance and walked over to him; he was sitting at the edge of the bed now. I stood between his legs and put my arms around his neck. I looked him straight in the eyes and said, "I love you, James."

He hugged me so tightly I couldn't breathe. "This was not the way I planned to say that to you."

I pulled his chin to make him look at me. "It was perfect timing." Then I gave him a soft kiss. He held me tight, and for the first time in my life, I truly felt safe and loved.

*James is **home** to me.*

***

"OH MY GOD! Lilly! When the hell were you going to tell us that you are pregnant?!?!?!" Annie yelled as she charged Lilly.

I stood there wide-eyed and mouth agape as I stared at Lilly's gigantic belly.

Aiden walked over to me and closed my mouth. "You okay, Christy? You act like you've never seen a pregnant lady before."

I shook my head and blinked a few times before Aiden came into focus. "Don't be silly, Aiden! Of course, I have seen a pregnant woman before! I was just shocked that you two idiots have been able to keep this quiet for—what?—six months?!" He laughed and grabbed some bags from me; we walked toward the kitchen where Annie had ushered Lilly to sit down.

"Hey, sweets!! Congratulations!! Why the hell have you been keeping this a secret?!" I hugged her tight! When I pulled back, Lilly was literally crying. "Oh gosh! I am so sorry! I didn't mean to yell at you! Are you okay? I'm not mad; I promise! Please don't cry!" Terrified, I looked at Aiden.

He laughed and walked over to us. "It's okay; it's the hormones. The further along the pregnancy gets, the more emotional she becomes. Isn't that right, honey?"

Lilly sniffled and looked up at me. "Sorry, Christy… I just thought back to the day I was going to video call you and Annie to tell you. It was the day Annie called me

302

to tell me you were shot. It was the worst time and the scariest news ever. Then, it just felt wrong to call and say, 'Hey, by the way, I'm pregnant; hope you're healing.' So we waited until now."

I hugged her again. "It's okay, Lilly. I am so happy for you both, and I cannot wait to meet this little one! We are going to be best friends! Just you wait! God kept me on this earth to meet this little lovebug!"

She cried again, but this time they were happy tears. "Tell me where you want me! What do you need help with to set up for the party?"

The next two hours went by quickly, and before we knew it, the doorbell was ringing. Annie ran out and started doing what she does best—hosting—this time for Lilly. The night was going by so quickly I almost didn't realize James had not arrived. I checked my phone and didn't have any missed calls or text messages. *Hmm. That's odd.*

I went to find Mikey. "Hey, have you seen or heard from James?"

He looked sheepish. "What's going on, Michael?" I only ever used his given name when I was losing my patience.

"Don't be upset, but there was a lead on Jenkins, so he went to the police station to check it out."

I saw red for a moment. *I cannot believe he is still doing this!* "Why does he insist on leaving me out of these things? I am the affected party, after all. Shouldn't I have a say or at least be kept informed?!"

Mikey pulled me into a bedroom and away from prying eyes. "Christy, he is just trying to protect you. We all are. I know it is not in your nature to let people take care of you, but James is a good man. He means well, and he is going to protect you at all costs. You have to decide if that is something you can live with. If it isn't, then maybe you need to walk away before you get in too deep." After his say, Mikey walked out.

The thing is, he wasn't wrong. I had been self-sabotaging relationships my entire life. This was probably the point at which the therapist I had in high school would say, "And why do you think that is?"

I went and sat on the chaise by the window and stared out at the moon. Admitting to you're the root of the problem is one thing, but acknowledging it to others and trying to work through it is completely another. If I were being honest, I didn't know if this was the time to try and work through my childhood trauma. Mikey knew what happened to me as a child. He knew why I rarely trusted people...and men even less. He had spent the better part of fifteen years proving to me that there are men who can be trusted and are good to their core.

I was stuck in my thoughts until I heard the door click. I snapped my head back and saw James walking toward me.

"Hey, I've been looking for you. Why are you crying?"

I hadn't even noticed I was.

He wiped my tears and kissed my forehead. I leaned into it, and he wrapped his arms around me. I am not sure how long we sat there like that, but then I heard him say, "Penny for your thoughts?"

I knew that this was not the best place to do this, but if I didn't do it now, I wouldn't do it at all. It wasn't fair to James; I had to tell him before we got further into this relationship.

I pulled away from James slightly so I could look up at him. "There is something I need to tell you. It is about my past. It may be a lot, so if at any point you feel like you need to stop me, please don't hesitate. Okay?"

He looked at me uncertainly. As if he had no idea how to respond. He blinked a few times and said, "I am here to listen. Anything you have to tell me, I will sit and hear you out. Always."

I smiled at him, but it was a lazy smile; there was no happiness behind it. James was a good man, but even good men have their limits. *Here's to hoping he's the exception.*

"Tanner Jenkins is a scumbag, but he is not the reason I have panic attacks. That night at your apartment, when I had my first panic attack, I told you it was because of Jenkins. And it wasn't a total lie. He was part of the reason, but not the main reason."

I paused and looked at James. He was tense, but while his posture was statue-like, his eyes were soft and encouraging.

"When I was fifteen, my mom was dating this guy. He was nice. He seemed to love my mom and always gave her pretty things. She fell hard for him. After a year of dating, he moved in with us. He and my mom developed a routine, and they learned to live together. I was a silent blip in the background. I mostly kept to myself, so it was easy to forget I was around. My mom was happy. She was living in bliss, and I was happy for her. Since she was always with him, I spent a lot of time with Mikey." I cleared my throat.

"After about a year of their so-called bliss, they started fighting. I have no idea what the fights were about, but one day I got home from school, and he was sitting on the couch with a gun in his hand. He waved it around while telling me to sit on the chair across from the couch. I was scared and looked around for my mom, but I didn't see her. Out of fear, I did what he asked." I paused.

This was the hard part, and I wasn't sure I could do it. I wasn't sure I could get the words out. I looked at James, and I could see his hands were clenched so hard I thought he might break a finger. It was as if he knew the next part was hard. He unclenched his hand and held on to mine. He didn't say anything though. I suppose it was his way of letting me know I could continue. So I did.

"'Where is mom?' I asked him. 'She's working, like always. Never has time for me anymore. I've got needs. I told her this, and she refuses to acknowledge that. So I'm going to have to just meet them myself. Maybe this way she'll take me seriously.' I had no idea what that meant, but I knew it wasn't good. So I sat there. Silent. Waiting for him to explain. He actually smiled at me at this point. It was the most disgusting smile I had ever seen, and I knew it was not good.

"He stood up and walked over to me, all the while pointing the gun at me. 'You know, you are your mom-ma's daughter. And today we are going to find out just how much you are alike.' I could feel the nausea rising, and I thought I might barf. He grabbed me by the arm and pulled me up from the chair. He held the gun to my side and told me to walk toward my mom's room. I couldn't move. He pushed me forward, and I stumbled, but he caught me and told me it would be worse if I fought. And for a second I believed him, so I walked.

"When we got to the bedroom he pushed me onto the bed and then got on top of me. I could feel his penis, and I just knew this was not going to end well. He used the gun to push up my blouse and pulled it off with his other hand. When he tossed it over the side of the bed he whistled and said, 'Damn, girl! You got better tits than your momma. I'm going to have fun with these.' He reached down and cupped my left breast. He pulled the bra down and played with my nipple. Then he leaned down and put his mouth on it while he pressed the gun to my side so I would stop squirming. I held still and retreated into my head as he continued to feel around and do things to me. While I was stuck in my head he took off my bra and pulled down my pants and underwear.

"Since I had not reacted for God knows how long, he thought I was done fighting it. So he set the gun down and worked on getting his pants and underwear off. He had to stand for this. When he got back on top of me and tried to put his dick inside, I shot him right in the chest. I didn't know Mikey was outside the door, but he ran in the house and busted the door down to find him on top of me. Mikey pushed him off and pulled the gun away from me. He called the cops, and he put a blanket over me.

"I didn't speak for months, but Mikey didn't give up on me. He got me to a therapist and stood by me every day and sometimes even nights. Mom refused to move or change the furniture. So every day for the next year, I had to relive that dreadful experience."

I paused and looked up at James. He was furious; I could tell. But the hand that was holding mine was still soft. He was fighting a battle within, and I was scared to say anything else. So I sat there and waited for him to process.

It took about thirty minutes before he said, "We should go home. It is getting late." He lightly pulled on the hand he was holding to get me to stand and walk with him.

I didn't know what he was thinking, but I felt that I could trust him, so I followed him. We said our goodbyes and headed to the penthouse.

Chapter 17

James had not said a single word since we left Lilly and
Aiden's house. He hadn't looked at me either, but neither
had he let go of my hand. Not even to get in the car. It's as
if my hand is keeping him grounded.

We reached the penthouse, and he pulled me toward
the couch in the living room. He sat on it and had me sit
on the coffee table across from him. This was the first time
in over an hour that he had looked directly at me.

"Thank you for trusting me. How I reacted was probably not what you expected. I am sorry that it has taken
me this long to say something. I wanted to react immediately, but I didn't want to say the wrong thing."

I blinked a couple of times because I could not believe
that he was apologizing for his reaction to the horrific

thing I just told him. He took my silence as permission to continue.

"Christy, it was self-defense. Nothing that happened that day or the events thereafter with your mother were your fault. I am only sorry that he got as far as he did. But, honey, I am so very proud of you!"

My eyes went wide. I had not expected this reaction at all, much less his kind words.

He let go of my hand and reached for my face. He caressed my cheek with one hand, and not until I leaned into it did he place his other hand on my other cheek. I looked at him, and he smiled at me.

"I love you, Christy Mills. Warts and all. There is nothing in your past or anything that you could do in the future that will change that. I can only pray that you believe me, but just in case, I will spend the rest of my life proving it to you." He leaned in and gave me the most gentle kiss I had ever experienced.

I cried. Not because I was sad, but because I could feel his honesty and intent in that kiss.

He finally came clean and told me about the break in the case. He shared the dossier with me, and it showed Jenkins at some abandoned warehouse in the worst part of town. It appeared to be where he had been hiding. In the file, there were multiple pictures taken at different times and on different dates. This scumbag had been lying low this whole time in that building. James said the police had it under control and would be raiding it tomorrow night.

After all that, we grabbed a snack and then made our way to bed. I couldn't sleep though. There were too many emotions lingering in my mind. I had not retold that story in a long time, and it had left me in a strange state of mind. Couple that with Jenkins, and I was in a pretty fucked-up place.

At 4:00 a.m., James had been asleep for a few hours. He was in REM sleep because his grip on my waist finally loosened, and he rolled over to his side of the bed. I jumped out of bed before he decided to roll back over. I headed for the spare room that had the belongings I had not yet unpacked. After about thirty minutes of rummaging, I finally found the box I was looking for.

There it was. My 9 mm semiautomatic pistol. I pulled it out and cleaned it. I found the ammo too. Once the gun was clean, I put it back in its holster and stuffed it into my gym bag with some new clothes on top of it.

Just before James woke up, I jumped in the shower and got ready for work. This would be much like most recent days, with the exception that I would be sneaking out of work to find this asshole and end this shit for good.

Mikey was supposed to ride to work with me, but it seemed that James messaged him last night and also switched around his personal schedule so he could accompany me. Supersweet gesture. I just wish I weren't lying to him.

When we reached the office, I took my usual route except, instead of heading to my office, I detoured into the women's bathroom. Christopher and Blake had added a private bathroom in my office when they remodeled, but I didn't want to be seen in the office. I changed out of my work clothes, holstered my pistol, and then made my way back out. I was able to sneak into the service stairwell, which led to the back alley.

Once I was out of the building, I made my way to the Metrorail. It was a short trip to the area where the warehouse was. It gave me time to plan while looking at the surveillance pictures. There was a fire escape that looked as if it could get me into the building from above. Hopefully, it would give me the advantage I needed. Daylight was not the best time to do this, but here I was acting irrationally and putting myself in harm's way to—what? Prove a point? To whom? Myself? Jenkins? God only knew.

I spent hours scouting the place. I made sure to stay out of sight as much as possible. Lord only knows if the cops were still out here surveilling. I didn't want to go inside if this idiot wasn't there. By now, I was certain that either James or Mikey was aware that I was not at work. Thankfully I slipped my phone onto Landon's desk before I left. Couldn't have James tracking my location. It was bad enough that I was out here looking for the very lunatic who tried to kill me. I can't have James or Mikey showing up, because then I will lose my nerve to confront Jenkins.

Around 4:00 p.m., Jenkins walked up to the building. He was a paranoid asshole. He kept looking over his shoulder and walking as if he were a psychopath, his back against the building wall.

I waited for him to get inside. Then I gave him another thirty minutes, just to be sure he wasn't coming back out. It didn't seem like it, so I made my way across the street and up the fire escape. I found an open window on the third floor. I wandered around the building until I found him on the first floor in the largest room.

This guy really was paranoid. He had a makeshift kitchen, bedroom, and toilet all in one place. Prison must have really done a number on him. I watched him from the far end of the room, outside of what appeared to be a side door. Poor bastard had no idea anyone was here.

I could honestly shoot him from here and jet, but truth was I wanted to speak to him. So I waited some more.

He finally lay down on the makeshift bed. This was my chance to get closer to him. His guard was down, and I could get the jump on him. As I made my way through all the crap in the room, I was able to hide behind what appeared to be a stove. His breathing appeared to be even. *Maybe he fell asleep? I'm not taking any chances.*

I pulled out the zip ties I picked up on the way. I rounded the edge of the stove and stood at the foot of the bed. He was definitely asleep. I tossed the zip ties on his chest and pointed my gun at his chest.

"Hey, douchebag! Wake up!"

He startled and tried to scramble. I fired a warning shot, and he stopped dead in his tracks.

"Not so fun being on the opposite end of the barrel, is it?" He looked at me with fear in his eyes. "Put those on."

I guess he didn't like being told what to do because his fear turned to rage. "Fuck you, bitch! I'm not doing that!"

I laughed. "Jenkins, the choice is yours. Do it and live. Don't do it and die. I can assure you, though, those will be the only choices you are getting today. What's it going to be?"

He spit at me, but it only reached the floor by my foot. I pointed the gun at his chest and put my finger on the trigger. His eyes widened, and he slipped the zip ties on.

Coward.

"FINE! What do you want?"

I looked at him, really looked at him. He'd changed over the years. He looked ashy and grey. It was the type of color that you see on people who are nearing death. Curiosity got the best of me. "Are you dying?"

His head snapped up. "Why the fuck do you care?"

I cocked my head to the side. "I don't. You just look like you're knocking on death's door. Are you?"

He fell to his knees and started coughing.

Huh. Guess he's a walking dead man. "Cancer?"

He looked up at me and simply nodded.

"I don't get it, Jenkins. If you are dying, why spend your days chasing and trying to kill me?"

He caught his breath before responding, "You already stole my life. This…This is just overtime. Seven months ago, docs said I only had six months to live. I figured I was already on my way out. Might as well take the bitch that took my life from me too." He coughed. "Do it. Shoot me. You'd be doing me a goddamn favor. I don't want to be here anymore." In the midst of a coughing fit, he continued in between each cough. "DO"—*cough*—"IT!" *Cough. Cough.*

I aim at him, but I can't bring myself to pull the trigger. I stand there with my pistol pointed at him, and all I can see is my mom's boyfriend's face. *I can't take another life. It's not worth it. I will lose myself; I'm sure of it.*

Before I could contemplate any further, there is a loud crash, and a SWAT team storms in. I drop my pistol and put my hands up. After securing the pistol, both Jenkins and I are handcuffed and walked outside. When we reach the patrol car, the detective on our case uncuffs me, and I see James and Mikey running toward me. I look over at the detective, and he nods at me.

I take off running toward them. They both grab me and hug me tightly. I have never been more happy to see men. These two are my safe place.

Epilogue

"Manhunt for Tanner Jenkins Comes to an End." That is the title on the newspaper this morning. James is in the kitchen with Annie; they're fighting over making waffles for me. Mikey, Lilly, Aiden, Blake, and Christopher are at the kitchen table, laughing and eating. I stand at the coffee bar, looking from side to side, and I can't help but admire the family I have built for myself over the years. We don't always get the family we want, but we always get the one we need.

"Stop, Annie! You are a guest! Let me make the damn waffles!" James snaps at Annie.

She turns to look at him and, in her very Annie way, sticks her tongue out at him and tells him to shove it.

We all laugh. Lilly stands and heads to the island to grab some eggs, but drops the plate halfway there. We all turn to look at her, and she is beet red.

"Shit, James! I'm sorry. I think I just peed on your floor."

Annie and Aiden run over, and Annie says, "No, Lilly, your water broke. You're having a baby!"

As we wait for Aiden to let us know what is going on, I ask James to get me a snack because I don't feel well. I attempt to get up and end up fainting.

Blink. Blink. Blink.

"What happened?"

James stands next to me. "You fainted, honey. I didn't think you were that hungry."

The doctor walked in. "Ah, you are awake. The good news is you are okay. The fainting was from lack of food. Your blood-sugar levels were low. You cannot let that happen again, Christy."

Puzzled, I looked at the doctor. "Doctor, I don't understand. I had a healthy dinner last night. I only missed breakfast by a few hours. How could my blood-sugar levels have dropped so quickly?"

He smiled at me. "It seems I will be the one to break the news to you. Is this your significant other?"

I looked at James, then back at the doctor, before nodding.

The doctor smiles again. "Christy, you are pregnant. I would like to do a sonogram to find out how far along you are, but if I had to guess, you are at least three to four months along for the lack of food to have such an effect on you."

I stared at him, my mouth agape.

James was the first to speak. "Doctor, are you certain?"

He pulled his glasses off and nodded at James. "As positive as I'll ever be. We did a blood test. Congratulations!"

Let's Connect

Get to know Maria Christina Benavides.

Instagram:
@maria_christina8

Milton Keynes UK
Ingram Content Group UK Ltd.
UKHW020930220424
441551UK00018B/1319